Some Western Shoshoni Myths

By

Julian Haynes Steward

First published in 1943

Published by Left of Brain Books

Copyright © 2023 Left of Brain Books

ISBN 978-1-397-66986-5

First Edition

PUBLISHER'S PREFACE

About the Book

"The Shoshone (also spelled Shoshoni) are Native Americans of the Great Basin region, and south and east of the Sierra Nevada mountain range. Shoshoneans are distributed widely--from Southern California, Death Valley and Mono Lake, through Utah to Western Colorado. Sacajawea, the woman who guided the Lewis and Clark expedition, was a Utah Shoshone.

While the beliefs of other Shoshonean tribes are fairly well documented, there is little published information about the mythology of the Great Basin Shoshone per se. This collection reveals that the Western Shoshone, who lived in central Nevada, were very similar to the Northern Californians in this regard. Their myths are inhabited by the lusty trickster Coyote, and other primordial zoomorphic demigods."

(Quote from sacred-texts.com)

About the Author

Julian Haynes Steward (1902 - 1972)

"Julian Haynes Steward (January 31, 1902 - February 6, 1972) was an American anthropologist best known for his role in the development of a scientific theory of cultural evolution in the years following World War II.

Steward was born in Washington, D.C. His father was the chief of the Board of Examiners of the U.S. Patent Office while his uncle was the chief forecaster for the U.S. Weather Bureau. While his father was a staunch atheist, his mother became a devout Christian Scientist. Steward showed no particular interest in anthropology as a child, but at the age of sixteen he enrolled at Deep Springs College, high in the south-eastern Sierra Nevada designed to produce future political leaders. His experience with the high mountains and local Shoshone and Paiute peoples awakened an interest in life in this area. After spending a year at Berkeley, Steward transferred to Cornell University. Cornell lacked an anthropology department, and he studied zoology and biology while the college's president, Livingston Farrand, continued to nurture his interest in anthropology. Steward earned his B.A. in 1925 and returned to Berkeley to pursue a Ph.D. in anthropology.

In 1935 Steward began a long involvement with the Bureau of Indian Affairs. He was key in the reform of the organization known as the New Deal for the American Indian, a restructuring which involved Steward in a variety of policy and financial issues. For the next eleven years Steward became an administrator of considerable clout, editing the Handbook of South American Indians. He also took a position at the Smithsonian Institution, where he founded the Institute for Social Anthropology in 1943. He also served on a committee to reorganize the American Anthropological Association and played a role in the creation of the National Science Foundation. He was also active in archaeological pursuits, successfully lobbying Congress to create the Committee for the Recovery of Archaeological Remains (the beginning of what is known today as 'salvage archaeology') and worked with Wendell Bennett to establish the Viru Valley project, an ambitious research program centered in Peru."

(Quote from wikipedia.org)

CONTENTS

INTRODUCTION

THESE myths were procured from several Shoshoni of Nevada and eastern California and from one Northern Paiute during 6 months' ethnographic field work [1] in 1935. They by no means exhaust the western Shoshoni mythological repertory, but, as this enormous area has heretofore been a blank on the ethnographic map, any material from it should be recorded.

The myths were recorded from the following localities and informants: Saline Valley, between Death Valley and Owens Valley, Calif.; Patsie Wilson, Shoshoni (now at Lone Pine), age about 50, informant; Andrew Gleim, interpreter. Panamint Valley, Calif.; George Hansen, age about 90. Upper Death Valley, Calif.; Bill Doe, Shoshoni (now at Beatty, Nev.), age about 70. Beatty, Nev.; Tom Stewart, Shoshoni, age about 70. Ash Meadows, Nev., where Shoshoni and Southern Paiute were somewhat mixed, but myths claimed to be Shoshoni; Mary Scott, age about 80. Lida, Nev.; John Shakespeare (now living at Cow Camp, near Silver Peak, Nev.), Shoshoni, age about 80. Big Smoky Valley, Nev.; Jenny Kawich (now living at Shurz, Nev.), Shoshoni, age about 65; these myths poorly remembered and very synoptic. Smith Valley, Nev., Tom Horn, Shoshoni, age about 60. Elko, Nev.; Bill Gibson, Shoshoni, age about 60. Winnemucca, Nev.; Charlie Thacker, Northern Paiute (now living at Owyhee, Nev.), age about 70. One myth is from the Gosiute

---

[1] This work was financed by the Department of Anthropology, University of California, and a grant-in-aid from the Social Science Research Council.

(who are really Shoshoni), procured in 1936 while doing field work for the Bureau of American Ethnology; informant, Müdiwak, age about 60.

There are few tales in this collection that are actually new. The themes, episodes, characters, and style are very similar to myths from Owens Valley and western Nevada, Paiute, from Owens Valley Shoshoni, from Ute and Southern Paiute, and from the Northern Lemhi Shoshoni.[1] Novelty lies only in local combinations of widespread elements and in local embellishment. Therefore, as the most interesting feature of Shoshonean mythology is local variation, an effort was made to obtain different versions of the same tale. From this standpoint, I was most successful in the Origin of People, procuring seven variants from as many localities. The Theft of Fire, the Theft of Pine Nuts, Coyote Learns to Fly, and Cottontail Shoots the Sun are also popular, wide-spread themes. The Race to Koso Hot Springs is an Owens Valley Paiute favorite. Other myths were collected at random.

Personal songs, sung by prominent myth characters, as in Owens Valley tales, seem to have been a general, though not important, feature of Shoshoni myths, but no effort was made to collect them.

---

[1] Steward, J. H., Myths of the Owens Valley Paiute, Univ. Calif. Publ. Amer. Archaeol. and Ethnol., vol. 34, No. 5, pp. 355-440, 1936. A few Shoshoni myths are recorded in the same, pp. 434-436. See also, Ethnography of the Owens Valley Paiute, same series, vol. 33, pp. 323-324, 1933; also, Lowie, R. H., Shoshonean Tales, Journ. Amer. Folk-Lore, vol. 37, pp. 1-242, 1924, and The Northern Shoshone, Amer. Mus. Nat. Hist., Anthrop. Pap., vol. 2, No. 2, pp. 233-302, 1909; also, Sapir, Edward, Texts of the Kaibab Paiutes and Uintah Utes, Amer. Acad. Arts and Sci., Proc., vol. 65, No. 2, pp. 297-535, 1930.

THE THEFT OF FIRE (SALINE VALLEY, CALIFORNIA. SHOSHONI)

A long time ago, the animals were people. They had no fire in any part of this country.

Lizard was lying in the sunshine. He saw a tule ash, blown by the south wind from a long way off, fall to the ground near him. All the people came over to look at it and wondered from where it had come.

They sent Hummingbird up into the sky to find out. They watched Hummingbird fly up. Coyote said, "I can see him. He is high in the sky." Lizard said, "I can see him sitting up there." They saw that Hummingbird looked all over to see from where the ash had blown. Coyote was watching him. He saw that Hummingbird looked to the south and saw something. Hummingbird came down and told the people that there was a fire in the south.

They all started toward the south. On the way, Coyote stationed the different animals at intervals. They went on until they could see the fire. The people there were having a big celebration and dance. Coyote made himself false hair of milkweed string. He joined the people and danced with them. As he danced he moved close to the fire and leaned his head over so that his hair caught on fire. As soon as it was lighted, he ran away. The fire in the camp went out, and the people began to pursue Coyote to recover their fire.

Coyote ran to the first man he had posted and passed the fire to him. This man ran with it to the next man, and in this way they passed it along. Every time the pursuers caught one of Coyote's people they killed him. There were fewer and fewer of them left, but they kept the fire.

At last only Rabbit remained. As be ran with the fire, he caused hail to fall to stop the pursuers. Rabbit cried as he ran. Rat, who was living alone on the top of a big smooth rock, heard Rabbit crying and went down to meet him. As he ran toward Rabbit, he tore the notch in the mountains near Lida. Rat took the fire from Rabbit and ran with it to his house, which was on the summit at Lida.

The pursuers gathered around his house, but could not get into it. They all died right there. They can be seen now piled on a mountain nearby.

Rat scattered the fire all over the country.

THE THEFT OF FIRE (PANAMINT VALLEY, CALIFORNIA. SHOSHONI)

THE birds and animals were men. At one time there was no fire in this country.

Lizard was lying in the sun to keep warm. As he lay there he noticed something falling slowly from the sky. When it came to the earth, all the people ran over and looked at it. They said, "What, is this?" Coyote said, "Don't you know what this is?" They said, "No." Coyote said, "This is an ash from a fire in another country. What are we going to do about it? Somebody must go far up in the sky to find out from where it came. Who can go?" Hummingbird said, "I can go."

Hummingbird started up in the sky, while everybody watched him. Coyote tipped his head and squinted one eye, watching him with the other. When Hummingbird was far up in the sky, Coyote saw him look toward the north, then turn and look toward the east. Then he looked toward the south, and, finally, turned toward the west. He continued to look a long time toward the west. Soon he came down.

When he was on the earth again, everybody gathered around him. Coyote said, "What about it? What did you see?" Hummingbird said that he had seen a. big body of water in the west. There were many people on the shore, dancing around a huge fire. Coyote said, "We must go over and get the fire."

They started toward the west. On the way Coyote stationed the people at intervals. When they got near the fire, Coyote made himself false hair out of string. There were many people dancing around the fire. Coyote joined them and began to dance, but they did not recognize him. All night as he danced, Coyote tried to catch the fire in his false hair. When it was nearly morning, he caught the fire and fled. The people had now lost their fire, and began to chase him.

Coyote ran to the first man he had posted and passed the fire on to him. This man ran with it to the next man, and in this way it was relayed from one to another until it was passed to Jackrabbit. Jackrabbit put it on his tail, making his tail black.

Rat had a house on the top of a tall rock with a smooth, vertical face. He sat in his house, while Jackrabbit was coming with the fire. The pursuers made hail fall. This hurt Jackrabbit so that he squealed as he ran. Rat heard this and came down to meet him. He took the fire from Jackrabbit, dodged his pursuers, and scrambled up to his house. The fire burned a red place on his breast.

The people below said, "Catch him, but do not kill him. We want the fire." Rat remained in his house and put the fire into a large pile of brush. The people below pleaded with him to give them some fire. Rat threw the brush in all directions. The brush now has the fire in it. You can get it out by making a fire drill of the brush.

THE THEFT OF PINE NUTS (SALINE VALLEY, CALIFORNIA. SHOSHONI)

THE people in this country had no pine nuts. They talked about going off toward the north to get some.

They started off toward the northeast. Coyote was among them. They went to a big camp where there were many people gathering pine nuts. Soon after they arrived, they began to play the hand game against these people. But the next day, they did not know whether they had lost or won. They went on to another place where there were also people who had pine nuts. Here they played a game of shooting at a small round target with a bow and arrow. They bet their lives in this game; the losers were to be killed by the winners. When one side missed the target, its opponents took its arrow. Crow was shooting and had only two arrows left. Coyote watched him. When Coyote saw him losing, he walked around and shouted and wondered what to do. Crow was about to shoot at the target again. Coyote said to him, "Why don't you hit the target?" Crow shot and missed. He had only one arrow now. When he shot this one, he hit the target. Then he began to win. He won back everything they had lost and then won everything the other people owned. Finally, their opponents even bet their pine nuts, and lost them.

The people did not want to give up their pine nuts. They hung them on a tall tree which had no branches, so that no one could climb up. During the night they slept under the tree to prevent anyone getting the pine nuts. Cottontail began to play his flute, "tu hu du du du . . . ." Some old women who were helping to protect the nuts knew that they were going to lose them and began to cry for help. Early in the morning, while the people under the tree were still asleep, Coyote and the others started to get the pine nuts. Coyote said, "What do these old women make a noise for? Why don't they go to sleep?" He poked their eyes with a stick and blinded them. Woodpecker (a red woodpecker) flew up in the tree and took the pine nuts.

When Woodpecker brought the pine nuts down, Coyote and the people took them and began to run for home. The others pursued them and caught those who became tired while they were running. They killed every one they caught. Although many people started out, nearly all were killed before they got home.

When nearly all the people were dead, Woodpecker gave the pine nuts to Crow. Crow went on with them. He hid them under his feathers, behind his ear, and in other parts of his body. The pursuers knew he would hide them this way and tried to hit him. They struck his leg and knocked it off. It went a long way through the air. Then they struck Crow and brought him to the ground. They said, "Now we will wait and take a rest."

After they had rested, they went on to where Crow had fallen and searched his body for the pine nuts. They found that Crow had left his feathers behind [i. e., shed his skin] and gone on, taking the pine nuts with him. They looked and a long way off saw where his leg had fallen, but Crow was far beyond, still carrying his pine nuts. They saw pine-nut trees all over the mountains, where the nuts had fallen from Crow's leg when it was knocked through the air. They saw smoke coming up through the trees, where the people were already out picking the pine nuts. Crow was flying about crying, "Caw, caw, I have had my pine nuts with me all the time."

All this happened up by Lida.

THE ORIGIN OF PEOPLE (SMITH VALLEY, NEVADA. SHOSHONI)

ALL the birds and animals were men. Yellowhammer and the others went to where some people up north had pine nuts. They had put their pine nuts in a deer-skin bag, hung high up on a white pine tree. Coyote's people played the hand game and other games with them. They played for many days and nights. They wanted the pine nuts. Mouse hunted, hunted, and hunted for the pine nuts, but did not see any. The people still played the hand game. Finally, Mouse found the deer-hide bag full of pine nuts hanging in the tree.

That night all the owners of the pine nuts went to sleep. During the night, Coyote and his people tried to get the pine nuts down. Coyote jumped, but he could not jump high enough. All the others tried, but none of them could jump high enough. Then Coyote asked Woodpecker to try. Woodpecker jumped, but he, too, failed to reach the bag of pine nuts. Then all the Woodpeckers took off their long beaks. Woodpecker took all these beaks and placed one upon another. The next time he jumped, he ripped open the deerskin bag and all the pine nuts fell down.

Coyote's people ate and ate. Finally, there was only one pin, nut left.

An old man went to the owners of the pine nuts and cried, "Wake up! Wake up! Someone is stealing your pine nuts!" They jumped up and ran after the others. As they caught each one of Coyote's people, they killed him. They killed many of them, but they did not find the pine nut. Coyote's people had relayed it along to the fastest runners. Coyote said, "Give me the pine nut. I can run fast." They gave it to Coyote. He carried it for a short distance and gave it to Crow.

Crow took the pine nut and bit the end off it. Then he hid it in his leg and ran. The pursuers were gaining on him. They shot him and killed him. When they came up to him, they kicked him, but his legs, ran on by itself, making a track to the mountains. All of Coyote's people were dead now.

By the time the pursuers arrived at the mountains, the pine nut trees had already grown. They grew all over the mountainsides. This was a long time ago. There are no pine nuts on the mountains up north where Coyote's people stole them. Only junipers grow there now.

THE THEFT OF PINE NUTS (ELKO, NEVADA. SHOSHONI)

AT one time there were no pine nuts in this country. All the pine nuts were up north, where Crane kept them on a high pole.

One day Crow, Coyote, Frog, Snake, Mouse, and all the other animals and birds were lying on a hill, looking down at some boys who were playing a game. Suddenly a puff of wind blew from the north and they could smell pine nuts cooking. They asked each other what the smell was. Coyote said, "It is pine nuts cooking." Crow said, "We will go up north and get them."

All the people started from somewhere south of Beowawee and traveled toward the north. They went past Owyhee and could smell the pine nuts in the north. On their way, they planned how they would get them. They traveled and traveled, many days. Some of the people got tired and stopped. Frog, Rattlesnake, and several others opt tired and could not go any farther. But the long-legged persons kept on going toward the north into what is now Idaho.

When Crow and the others got to Crane's place, where the pine nuts were, they suggested that everybody have a round dance. They all began to dance; they danced all night, until sunup. The girls at Crane's place talked about the different men. They said, "Look at Coyote. He is a bad man. He is ugly. Look at Skunk." They turned Skunk over and said, "He is a pretty boy. White Mouse and White Weasel are pretty boys, too." Everybody did the round dance. After while they stopped to eat. When they did this, Weasel and Mouse went away to hide; they went to sleep.

When morning came, all the people played the hand game. They played for bows and arrows, feathers, and other things. They played all day. Weasel and Mouse did not join the game because they were sleeping.

That night all the people did the round dance again. Mouse and Weasel came to the dance, but, after the people had eaten, went away to sleep. Everyone danced the round dance for 5 nights and played the hand game every day. By the time it was all over, they all went to sleep.

An old woman had been guarding the pine nuts. Mouse and Weasel tried to get the nuts, but they were tied on the top of a high pole and could not be reached. They took two woodpecker beaks, tied them together, and shot them at the pine nuts. All the pine nuts fell down. Crow and his people took the pine nuts and ran toward the south. When this happened, the old woman hollered, clapping her hand over her mouth. Crane woke up, and told his people to chase the thieves. They could see them running in the distance.

Crow saw that Crane and his people were pursuing them. A small bird among Crow's men tried to carry the nuts, but they were too heavy for him. Crane's people overtook Crow's people and killed them. Only Crow and Coyote remained. Coyote took some of the nuts. While he ran, he chewed them up and spit them out everywhere. Pine nut trees grew up wherever he spit. Crow also took some and put them in his leg. Then he sat down on the saddle of a hill. Crane saw Crow put the pine nuts under his arm and in his leg, and, when he came up to Crow, kicked and killed him. When he kicked Crow, the nuts were scattered all over the mountains. Then Crane looked and saw that the mountains were all black with smoke from places where the people were roasting pine nuts. [1]

Crane took his two children to a place where there was smoke, hoping to get some pine nuts to eat. It was Crow's mother's camp. When she saw Crane coming, she said, "I will give Crane all the wormy ones." When Crane came up to her, she said, "I will open some good, fresh pine nuts for you." She opened one and it was full of worms; the next one had worms too. She opened one after another and they all had worms.

Crane gave up trying to get pine nuts and said, "I will go down by the river and stay there." When Crane flew away, Crow's mother tried to strike him, but only knocked off his tail. That is why cranes have short tails.

Kaŋgwüsi gweak: [2] (Woodrat's tail, pulled off).

---

[1] B. G. believes that because of Crow's part in procuring pine nuts, crows should not be killed today.

[2] The conventional myth ending, meaning, in effect, "It is finished."

THE THEFT OF PINE NUTS (WINNEMUCCA, NEVADA. NORTHERN PAIUTE) [1]

THE north wind was blowing and Coyote could smell pine nuts. Coyote said, "It smells good. I will find the pine nut eaters." He traveled to where people were eating pine nuts. They were making mush of them. The people said, "Don't make the mush too thick. Put plenty of water in it. There is a stranger here. We don't know what he wants. Don't put coarse nuts in the mush. He may steal them."

Coyote came back and told his own people about it. He said, "Those people have fine food. I ate some soup. They made me some thin mush without any whole pine nuts in it, so I could not steal them. Hurry, pack up and we will go after them."

Coyote and his people started out to steal the pine nuts. Everybody--Chipmunk, Magpie, Chickenhawk, Mouse, Hawk, Skunk--everybody went. They were all people. [When they arrived] they gambled with the people in the north. Coyote said, "Mouse, you look for the pine nuts, while we play the hand game. They are hidden." Coyote told him to find the whole ones. Mouse was small and could get into small places. While they were playing the hand game, Mouse found the nuts under a house and started to run home with them. All Coyote's people ran to help him.

---

[1] Although this story is known throughout the Basin, it is here told at the northern limit of pine nuts. The people to the north actually do not have pine nuts in their territory and it may well be in such a place that the story originated.

The northern people followed. They killed Coyote first. Then they killed the others. They cut each person open to find the pine nuts. [But before each person was overtaken] he had relayed the nuts to another. Finally, Rotten-legs (Hawk) was the only person left. He had the pine nuts in his leg. They cut Rotten-legs open, but did not find anything. His leg stunk so bad that they threw it away toward the south.

The people saw smoke in the hills. [1] The pine nuts [which had been scattered when the leg was thrown] grew fast. There used to be pine nuts in the north, but now they are all gone. They grow around Winnemucca now.

---

[1] This smoke was presumably from the fires of people cooking pine nuts, though it is not explicitly explained In this myth.

THE ORIGIN OF PEOPLE (PANAMINT VALLEY, CALIFORNIA. SHOSHONI)

THE earth was covered with water. The water dried up quickly. At this time the birds and animals were men.

Coyote was walking along the Panamint Mountains, when he saw a very beautiful woman who had very white skin. Her name was pabon' posiats, "tan louse." She was carrying a jug of water. Coyote followed her, and when he came up to her, he said, "I am very thirsty. Give me a drink of water." She pointed to a place (about one-half a mile away) and told him to go over there, and she would give him a drink. Coyote did so. When she came up to him, she again pointed to a distant place and told him to go there. In this way she continued to put him off until they reached her home.

The girl lived with her mother. The mother said to her, "Where did you get him?" Coyote went to some water and started to drink. While he was drinking the girl tried to strike him several times, but Coyote dodged each time. Then she said to him, "You go into the house," pointing to a big hole in the house. Coyote went in, and saw many bows and arrows around the walls of the house. [1]

---

[1] The inference is that these weapons belonged to men who had previously visited her and whom she had killed.

During the night Coyote's advances toward the women were frustrated [1] . . . In the morning Coyote asked the woman who owned the bows and arrows. She told him to take them and to hunt some ducks. That day Coyote killed ducks and caught fish, which he brought back to the house.

In the evening the women cooked the ducks. They ate some and disposed of some . . .

That night Coyote made advances to both the girl and her mother . . . By morning the girl's belly was large. She began to bear children, putting them into a large basketry water jug. She told Coyote that they were his babies. When Coyote was ready to leave, the girl said to him, "Carry the babies in the jug. These babies will cry for water, but you must be careful. If you give them water, open the stopper only a little or they will get out." She showed him how to give them water.

Coyote started out carrying the jug, which was very heavy. As he went along, the babies cried, "I want water. I am dry!" Coyote said, "They are thirsty; maybe they will die." Coyote opened thejug, and the babies all ran out. They went in all directions. [2] The boys fought among themselves with bows and arrows. These people became the different Indian tribes.

---

[1] In this and in subsequent versions of this tale, the familiar vagina dentatum theme is used to explain the failure of Coyote's amorous advances. Coyote remedies the situation by using a piece of wood or mountain sheep neck. The theme also is made to account for the disposition of part of the food eaten by the women. Deletions of this material are indicated by dots.

[2] G. H. added that some paper was lost at this time, implying that the Indians had known how to write, but that the art was lost when Coyote opened the jug.

THE ORIGIN OF PEOPLE (DEATH VALLEY, CALIFORNIA. SHOSHONI)

COYOTE had a home. He hunted rabbits to make a rabbit-skin blanket. When he had a great many skins, he started to make the blanket in his house. While he was working on his blanket, he saw a shadow pass the door. He went out of the door to see what it was, and saw a woman running. She had a rabbit's tail on her buttocks. He chased the woman, and she ran toward the west. Coyote ran fast, but could get no closer to her. He chased her to the ocean. [1]

At the edge of the ocean the woman stopped and sat down. She said, "I will lie on my back and swim across, and carry you over." They started across, the woman carrying him. When they had gone a little way, Coyote moved down on her. The woman dumped him off into the water. Coyote had already decided that, if she put him off into the water, he would turn himself into a water skate ("some little long-legged insect that runs on the water"). When she pushed him into the water, he turned into the skate and crossed the ocean. He reached the other side before the woman.

When Coyote got to the other side he found a tree and made himself a bow. He took green stringy stuff from the water, which he put on the back of his bow instead of sinew. He made the bow string of the same thing. Then he found some cane,

---

[1] The informant's English term. The Shoshoni word would probably be translated "large water," i. e., "lake."

made arrows, and began to shoot ducks. He took the ducks to the woman's house.

There were two women living at this house, the woman he had followed and her mother. [1] The women were sitting outside their house. They told Coyote to go inside and sit down. When Coyote went in, he saw quivers made of fox skin hanging all over the wall. [2]

The women started to cook the ducks. They ate the ducks; both women ate. Coyote was singing. He made a hole in the house and watched the women. After eating the meat, the women disposed of the bones. . . . Both of them did this.

They went into the house to sleep. Coyote made advances to the woman he had pursued. He was frustrated . . . In the morning, Coyote went out and got a hard stick. It was a kind of hard sage brush. He hid it by the house . . . The next morning, Coyote hunted mountain sheep. He killed a small one and took the bone from its neck. He put the neck bone by the house in the same place he had hidden the stick. . . . He made successful advances that night . . .

In the morning, both women were large in the belly. The older one started to weave a basketry water jug. She finished making the jug. Both women put their babies in the jug. When they had finished, they told Coyote to go back home and to take the jug full of babies with him. Coyote started. When he came to the ocean, the old woman put a flat stick across it and Coyote walked over on it. He came toward his home. He went to Owens Valley.

---

[1] They were given no names.
[2] No mention here is made of the owners of the quivers.

While he was carrying the jug, he heard a noise. He wondered what it was. He pulled the stopper out of the jug. Indians came out; many Indians. When only a few were left inside the jug, he put the stopper back. The woman had told him to pull it out when he came to the middle of the world, but he had pulled it out when he heard the noise. He put the stopper in again and came on to Death Valley. In Death Valley he pulled it out again, and the remaining Indians came out. They stayed here. That is why there are Indians here now.

THE ORIGIN OF PEOPLE (BEATTY, NEVADA. SHOSHONI)

EVERY day Coyote met a girl. The girl lived with her mother, who said, "Why don't you bring that Coyote here? He will hunt, game for us. Bring him home."

When Coyote met the girl again, he became amorous. She said, "All right, but I shall go a little way ahead. Then you come." The girl went some distance toward the east and stopped. When Coyote came up to her he said, "This is the place." She said, "No, it is farther." She went ahead again, and when Coyote cattle to where she was, the same thing happened. Every time he came up to her, Coyote made advances. Thus, they went from place to place and crossed a high mountain.

While crossing the mountain, they came to a cliff. What Coyote discovered while climbing the cliff . . . frightened him. Coyote continued to follow the, girl, and they went toward the east, where the girl and her mother had a house.

Coyote and the girl reached the house. That night the girl's Mother, an old woman, cooked all kinds of food for them to eat.

She said to Coyote and the girl, "You go and make a bed outside." Coyote . . . knew what to expect . . . He was frustrated.

In the morning the old woman said to Coyote, "You go and hunt ducks. There are a lot of arrows out there. Take them with you. Hunt all day and kill many ducks."[1]

Coyote hunted all day and brought back a great many ducks. The old woman plucked them and boiled them in a pot. She and her daughter ate the meat. Coyote sat to one side. He could see how they disposed of the bones . . .

That night Coyote's advances were frustrated . . .

In the morning the old woman said to Coyote, "You go and hunt again. Hunt mountain sheep. There are arrows outside. Take them with you." Coyote said, "I am a great hunter. All right. I will go and hunt."

Coyote walked up into the mountains. Coyote was a smart man. Halfway up the mountain, he saw a mountain sheep. It was young and small and had short horns that were still soft and weak. Coyote went after the small sheep and killed it at once. He shot it. He butchered it and prepared it. He wanted a piece of the neck, because the neck is strong. He cut off a piece of the neck and said, "I do not want to give this to those women." He hid it.

Coyote went back to the women's house that night. The old woman met him and took the sheep. She looked it over and said, "Coyote, what did you do with that neck?" Coyote, said, "I threw it away." The old woman said, "It is good to eat." The old woman and the girl boiled the meat. They ate it, and when they were through it was dark.

---

[1] T. 8. did not know the source of these arrows, but supposed that the old woman had made them.

The old woman said, "You two make a bed." The girl made a bed. Coyote was still lustful. The girl was very fine; she was a good looking girl . . . Coyote went to where he had hidden the mountain sheep's neck. He returned bringing it with him . . . He visited both the girl and the old woman . . .

In the morning, Coyote went out to hunt ducks. He brought back a great many ducks for the women to eat. The women plucked and boiled the ducks. They ate off the meat, then pulverized the bones with a rock.

That night Coyote again visited the women.

The old woman made a basketry water jug, a very large jug. She worked on it for several days. Coyote stayed with the women. Every day he hunted.

After a few days, the old woman said to him, "You must go home. Carry that jug, with you. Don't open it while you are traveling. Don't open it anywhere. When you come to the middle of the country, open it."

Coyote started out carrying the jug, but it was too heavy. He said, "What is in this jug? It is too heavy. I want to open it and see what is in it." He decided to open it. He took a rock and hammered open the stopper. At once people jumped out. Many people jumped out. Nearly all the people jumped out. There were young men and young women. These were fine looking men and women. This happened near Saline Valley. [1]

When only a few people remained in the jug, Coyote put the stopper back in. He carried the jug on his back and went on

---

[1] These are Shoshoni.

toward his own country. When he had gone half way, he opened it again. This was at Owens River. [1] Old and homely people came out. A great many people came out. Then Coyote threw away the jug.

That is how men and women were made.

---

[1] These are Northern Paiute.

THE ORIGIN OF PEOPLE (ASH MEADOWS, NEVADA. SHOSHONI)

ONE day, Coyote went out to hunt rabbits. While he was hunting, he saw a large naked woman in the distance. This excited him. He said to himself, "Whew, I have never seen a woman like that. I will follow her." He followed her for a long time, but could not quite overtake her. He followed her over many mountains. When he came to White Mountain [Fish Lake Valley], he was very thirsty. He saw that the woman was carrying a tiny basketry water jug, and he asked her for a drink. She gave him the little jug, and he drank and drank, but still there was water left in it. Then she walked on, and he followed her.

Finally, they came to a large lake of water. The woman said, "My home is over there." She crossed the lake on top of the water. Coyote said, "I cannot do that. I will walk around." The woman turned and gave Coyote the legs of a water bug [skate?] that runs on the top of the water. Coyote followed her over to her house.

The woman lived in a house with her mother, who was called tsutsip^{ü}, "ocean," maa'puts, "old woman." She was like Eva, the first Woman. Eva had never seen a man before. In the morning, Eva got up very early and began to weave a fine, big water jug. Coyote stayed with the women for several days.

One day Coyote went hunting for deer. He wondered what was the matter [with the women] . . . He asked his stomach, his ears, his nose, and his foot what was the matter. None of them could tell him. Then a white hair on the end of his tail said, "You are just like a little boy. Take a neck bone . . . and use that."

Coyote did this . . .

Coyote went out to hunt. The old woman had nearly finished her big water jug. The two women told each other that they were pregnant. When the jug was finished, they gave birth to many tiny babies, all like little dolls, and put them in the jug.

When Coyote returned, they said to him, "Maybe your brother, Wolf, is lonesome for you. We want you to go back home." Coyote said, "All right, I will go." Eva then said to the children, "You have no home here. You must go with Coyote." She put the basket of children on Coyote's back, and told him to carry it with him. It was very heavy, but Coyote said that he had carried deer down from the mountains on his back, so that he was strong and did not object.

The women instructed Coyote about the jug. They said, "When you come to Saline Valley, open the stopper just a little way, then replace it quickly. When you come to Death Valley, open it a little more. At Tin Mountain (Charleston Peak) open it half way. When you are in Moapa, take the stopper out all the way." Coyote said he would do this.

Coyote carried the jug along, but soon became very tired and could scarcely hold it. When he arrived in Saline Valley, he opened the stopper a little way. Tall, dark, handsome men and girls jumped out and ran away. These were the best looking people in the jug. This frightened Coyote, but he put the stopper back, and picked up the jug. In Death Valley, he opened it again. Here, more handsome people jumped out and ran away. The girls all had long, beautiful hair. When he came to Ash Meadows, he opened it. The Paiute and Shoshoni came out.

These people were fine looking, too. At Tin Mountain, Coyote let some fairly good people out of the jug. When he opened it in Moapa, very poor, short, ugly people came out. The girls here had short hair with lice in it. All the people had sore eyes. That is the way the are now.

This is the way Eva had her first children. Coyote was the father.

THE ORIGIN OF PEOPLE (BIG SMOKY VAL-LEY, NEVADA. SHOSHONI)

WOLF had a big water jug. He said to his brother, Coyote, "Coyote, don't touch or open this jug. Be careful!" Then Wolf went away. Coyote said, "What is the matter with my brother? What is in that jug? Why did he tell me not to open it? I am going to open it." Coyote pulled out the stopper.

Many people came out and flew away. [1] He replaced the stopper, while a few remained. The good ones had come out and had flown away like flies.

Wolf told Coyote they were going to move. He told Coyote to carry the big jug. They went to Smoky Valley. Wolf did not know that Coyote had opened the jug. He thought all the people were still in. When they came to Smoky Valley, Wolf said, "Open that jug!" Just a few Indians came out. They are the Shoshoni.

---

[1] "Flew away" is probably the informant's confusion, rather than part of the native tale. In fact, this legend is not only synoptic, but probably incomplete.

THE ORIGIN OF PEOPLE (SKULL VALLEY, UTAH. GOSIUTE)

TWO women, a mother and her daughter, lived on an island in Great Salt Lake ...

Sinav and Coyote lived in Skull Valley. After the girl had killed all the men in the world, she came to get Coyote. Sinav told her that there was no [such person as] Coyote.

Sinav went with the woman toward her home. It was very hot and they had no water. After a while the woman wanted to rest under a tree but Sinav knew better [than to let her stop]. He said, "No, we must go on." They went on to Great Salt Lake. The woman walked across on the water to the island. Sinav stayed near the shore, standing in the water. The girl's mother said to her, "Why don't you bring him over?" The girl made a path of earth through the water. Sinav walked over to the island, the water closing in behind him all the way. [1]

Sinav went hunting and brought back deer. The women ate the meat and disposed of the bones . . . Sinav killed two mountain sheep, an old one and a young one. He first used the neck of the old one . . . Then he used the neck of the young one . . .

For several days Sinav hunted and brought in two deer each day. Each night he visited the women. Each woman bore a baby

---

[1] This is probably Antelope Island, which, in years of exceptionally low water, is joined to the mainland.

daily and put it in a large basketry jug. The jug became larger each day.

Finally, the older woman told Sinav to go South and take the jug with him. She made a path of dirt across the lake to the shore. Sinav crossed, and the water closed in behind him. At first, as he walked along, the jug was light and easy to carry. It became heavier. After a while, he had to set it down. He went on again and set it down again. Each time he went a shorter distance before he had to set it down. This happened five or six times.

Sinav heard a buzzing noise like a bee inside the jug. He wanted to look. When he began to open it, men jumped out and made a lot of dust. They knocked him over and ran away. Three times he removed the stopper and people came out. He watched them. They ran in all directions. They were the Shoshoni, Ute, Paiute and other tribes. The last man to come out was all covered with dust' He was the Gosiute.[1]He is tougher than ther people; he is bulletproof.

---

[1] This is probably Antelope Island, which, in years of exceptionally low water, is joined to the mainland.

THE RACE TO KOSO HOT SPRINGS (DEATH VALLEY, CALIFORNIA. SHOSHONI)

AT one time many people lived at Koso Hot Springs. These were animals who were then people. Even Sun was a person. Bear and all kinds of animals were there.

The people were going to have a race. In this race they bet themselves [that is, their lives]. Two of them made a fire to cook those who lost the race. One of the firemakers was Mudhen. [1]

Every one went south to a place where there were some willows. Coyote was with them. Many people, who were going to race, gathered there. When the race started, Coyote walked off to the willows and began to eat a white sugar [sap] on the stems. Frog went to Coyote and struck him. Coyote came out of the willows, and found that all the people had gone. He started to run; he was way behind them. As he ran he saw Frog ahead of him, sitting down. Coyote stopped and urinated on Frog. Then he went on. Soon he saw Frog ahead of him again sitting down. Again he urinated on Frog and ran on. The people were getting close to Koso Hot Springs. While they ran, Frog jumped over Coyote and urinated on him. The people were near Koso Hot Springs. Frog got there first and won the race. After the race, the firetenders threw the losers into the fire. Only Bear and Sun remained. When they started to drag Bear to the fire, he roared, but they threw him into it. Only Sun was left. The

---

[1] Possibly hell-diver, a bird which has a red eye, said to have been caused by making the fire. B. D. doesn't remember who the other firemaker was.

people started to talk about Sun. They said, "We had better leave him so that there will be light." Coyote, who was chief, said, "If he had beaten me, he would have thrown me into the fire. We must throw him in." Coyote took hold of Still. When he did this, Nighthawks, Chipmunks, and all the other people ran for the house. [1] Coyote dragged Sun to the fire. His friends were afraid that it would be dark; they ran to the house. When Coyote was ready to throw Sun into the fire, he looked to see which way he would have to run to get to the house. Then he pushed Sun into the fire and all went dark. Coyote ran toward the house but could not find it. He ran around looking for it and shouting. The people in the house heard him, but would not answer. Coyote looked all around, shouted, but heard no answer. He found a flat stick, a kind of paddle, and knew that he was near the house. He said to himself, "I am here." He had climbed over the house many times before, but had not known where he was.

All this had happened in the fall, and Coyote had traveled around all winter looking for the house. He became thin. In the spring he was still looking for the house. While he was looking, the people inside talked about him. They said, "We had better tell him to come here. He is smart. He might tell us what to do." After this, they answered Coyote when he shouted. Coyote went inside the house. While he was crawling in, Chipmunk sat by the door. Coyote put his hand on Chipmunk and said, "I am putting my hand on my brother-in-law." He went on into the house.

Owl and Nighthawk went out into the darkness to get green plants to eat. They did not give any to Coyote. Coyote heard them chewing, and said, "What are you people eating?" They

____

[1] In other versions, Coyote had allowed his people time to build a house before throwing Sun Into the fire.

put some of it into Coyote's mouth. Coyote said, "I don't want you to do that." They said, "We have been eating that kind of stuff (tuhuvida)."

Coyote started to talk. He said, "We had better start to make the sun. There are a lot of different kinds of people here. Some of us ought to know how to make the sun." The people said, "That is fine." Some of them started to shout, and a little light appeared. Nighthawk wanted it all dark, because he traveled at night. All the people were there. Coyote said, "When I shout, the sun will come out." Coyote shouted and it became completely dark again. Woodpecker and Mallard Duck were there. They shouted, and the sun came out. After this, the people came out and found that there were many green plants everywhere.

Coyote started to eat tuhuvida. Coyote said, "I am going to make it sweeter," and urinated on it. [1] After this, some of the people tasted it. It had been sweet before, but Coyote made it salty and bitter.

------

[1] Tuhuvida, some kind of plant with yellow flowers. It was sometimes eaten by Shoshoni, but has an unpleasant flavor for which Coyote is held responsible.

THE RACE TO KOSO HOT SPRINGS (SALINE VALLEY, CALIFORNIA. SHOSHONI)

ALL the animals were down south somewhere (pitiwana). All of them--Crow, Badger, Lizard, Coyote, the birds--were racing against Sun. Frog was in the lead, and reached Koso Hot Springs before Sun. When he got there, he waited for the other animals to arrive.

When all the animals had arrived, they built a large house for all the people. They all went into the house and left Coyote to throw Sun in the fire. Before Coyote did this, he looked carefully to see where the house was. Then he threw Sun into the fire and all became dark. This is why the springs are hot now.

Coyote set out for the house in the darkness, but could not find it. He searched all over for it. He wandered around for a year. He was very thin by this time.

The people in the house began to talk about Coyote. They said he was the smartest of them all; they wanted him. They began to look for him, and found him close by. It was springtime. Coyote was very thin. The people brought him into the house and gave him a corner in which to rest.

The people wanted Sun back. They asked each other how they could get Sun again. Mallard Duck said, "Quack, quack, quack," and every animal made his noise, trying to bring Sun back. When Mallard quacked, a little light, like dawn, began to show. They asked Coyote to make his noise; when he did so it went dark again. Duck quacked again, and it began to get light. The third time Duck quacked, Sun came out. The people saw that it was springtime; everything was green. They went out of the house.

Sun was close to the earth. They killed him, took his gall out, and threw it high in the sky.

COYOTE LEARNS TO FLY; THE ORIGIN OF PEOPLE (SALINE VALLEY, CALIFORNIA. SHOSHONI)

COYOTE had a house in Saline Valley where he lived alone. He decided to make a basket and he went out to gather willows. He did this for many days. While he was gathering the willows he heard a sound but did not know what caused it. He said, "Oh, what was that noise I just heard?" There were green blowflies all over Coyote. The flies buzzed so loudly he could not hear the noise. . . . He killed them. After he had killed all the flies he knew what the noise was. It was somebody singing. Then Coyote began to sing and dance, carrying all his basket willows. He said, "Maybe I am going to be a doctor."

While he danced, he heard someone laughing at him. He looked up in the air and saw that Geese were laughing. He said, "What are you fellows, my brothers, doing up there?" Geese said, "We are going to eat eggs." Coyote said, "I think I will go along with you fellows." He dropped the basket willows and ran along under the Geese.

After a while, the Geese rested on the ground to wait for Coyote. They said, "We had better give some feathers to Coyote." When Coyote overtook them, each one gave him a feather. After this, they pointed to a mountain some distance off and said, "You fly around that hill and try your feathers." Coyote put on the feathers, and flew away saying, "Wo' wo' wo'." The Geese told Coyote to land on a certain mountain top and face them. But he lighted on it. with his back to them. The

Geese did not like to have Coyote's back to them. It made them angry.

Coyote left the mountain and walked back to the Geese. They were angry and killed him. They smashed his head with a rock. Then they flew away toward the east (Hauta). Coyote lay dead.

When Coyote came to life again, he stretched and placed his hands behind his head. His fingers felt his brain, which was running out of his skull. He said "My brothers have left me something to eat," and he began to eat, thinking his brains were food they had given him. Then he got up and found that he had been eating his own brains. He said, "I was eating my own brain," and vomited.

Then Coyote looked for the Geese. He saw them way over the mountains, toward the east. Coyote picked up some rocks and put them into his head, in place of the brains he had eaten, and started after the Geese. He went to the top of the mountain where he had seen the Geese, and saw that they were over the next mountain to the east. He went on to that mountain, and saw that they were over the next one to the east. In this way, Coyote kept going until he came to the shore of the ocean.

Here he saw many people, lying scattered on the shore, with their faces down. They were all dead. He turned over each one to look under him for eggs, but the Geese had eaten all of them.

One woman was lying at some distance from the others; she had one egg. Coyote cut her open, and found a girl baby. He said to the baby, "You are going to be my sister." Then he said, "You are going to be my baby." Coyote got himself some clay and made himself like a woman, with all the parts. He built a fire and steamed himself, as women do after childbirth. After this he drank only warm water. In this way Coyote made himself into a woman to nurse and care for the baby.

Coyote started back for her old home, carrying the baby on her back. While she traveled along, the baby became bigger each day. As the girl rapidly grew bigger, Coyote began to remove the clay which he had used to make himself into a woman. He changed himself back into a man, for the girl had grown very large. He said to her, "You will be my wife." But the girl said to him, "When you first cut open the woman and found me as a baby, you called me sister." Coyote said, "No, I called you my wife then." The girl said, "No you didn't, you called me sister." Coyote said, "No, I called you my wife." Coyote liked that girl.

Coyote and the girl stayed together that night. She became pregnant at once. They traveled on toward this country. A baby was born on the trail. Coyote began to weave a water jug. When he finished it, he put the baby inside. His wife disappeared, and Coyote came home alone, carrying the jug with the baby inside.

When Coyote arrived in his own country, he set the jug down. Out came dozens of boys and girls, fully grown, walking by themselves. The first to come out were fine looking, but they had no bows and arrows. They started off toward the north, running and raising a big dust. Coyote shouted, "Wait! I want to pick some of the best ones for my people." Fine looking people without bows and arrows also ran across the mountains to the west. Those that went toward the east (süvü watü nümü) were scrubby people, and carried bows and quivers full of arrows. Those who went south were also scrubby, and had bow and arrows. These were Coyote's people, the Shoshoni. Those who went north, settled at different places along Owen's Valley. They were the Northern Paiute.

If Coyote had not found a live egg on the shore of the ocean, there wouldn't be any people.

COYOTE LEARNS TO FLY; COYOTE BECOMES A MOTHER (ASH MEADOWS, NEVADA. SHOSHONI)

WOLF'S younger brother was Coyote. One day Coyote was hunting on the other side of the hills, east of the Armagosa Desert. Near Manse he saw a man going south and began to follow him. After a while he came to a place where there are rows of rocks which look like white geese resting on fine, white earth. These were Swans who were sitting and smoking.[1]

When Coyote came to the Swans, he said, "I want to go with you fellows." The Swans offered him some of their feathers. They put them along his arms and legs, and told him to try them out. They said, "You fly to that little hill. Don't go too far. Go around it once and come back." Coyote agreed to do that. They asked him how he felt. He said, "I feel fine." He flapped his new wings, shouted, and commenced to fly. He flew around the hill twice. This made the Swans very angry; they scolded him when he returned. They smashed his head with a large flat rock, then flew away to the west.

When the Swans were over the mountains to the west, Coyote woke up and said, "Where are those men? There is no one here." He saw only the white rocks on the ground. Then he saw the Swans in the sky over the mountains to the west, and began to follow them.

---

[1] it is not clear whether the rocks were swans, or whether there was a swan opposite each rock. Probably these were geese, not swans.

When he reached the top of the mountains where he had seen them, they were over the mountains bordering Saline Valley. He went on, but by the time he came to those mountains, the Swans were over the Inyo Mountains. He continued to follow them, but when he came to the Inyo summit, they were over the Sierra Nevada range.

When Coyote reached the summit of the Sierra Nevada Mountains, he saw no one. To the west there was nothing but water. He walked around wondering what to do. He saw some people camping near the edge of the water. He went down to see them and found that they were all dead. There were dead men, women, and babies. They had been killed by the Swans.

While he was looking at the dead people, he found a woman with a baby part way out of her chest. The baby was crying. Coyote pulled the baby all the way out, and said, "What am I going to do?" He asked his stomach what to do, but his stomach said nothing. He asked his ears, but they merely straightened up. He asked his nose, but it said nothing because it only had a big hole at the end. He asked his mouth, but it merely drew back into a grin. He asked his foot, but the toes pinched up together. He said, "Hurry up! Tell me, the baby is crying. What shall I do?" He asked his tail. The tail straightened up, and a white hair on the tip of it stood up, and said, "You are foolish! Fix that baby! Make a fire and heat some water. Wash the baby and tie up its navel, or the blood will all run out. Tie it up with buckskin. Get some white clay, Coyote, and make yourself breasts and nipples. Steam them in the fire and they will become full of milk. Then give some to the baby. Tonight dig a hole and build a fire in it. Heat five little rocks and put them in it. Cover it up with brush and earth, then lie on it. That will be good for your blood. Later on, people will do this way. In the morning, wash the baby. Stay here 5 days, and then the afterbirth will come out." Coyote did as he was told. He stayed there 5 days and took care of the baby.

After this, Coyote decided to go home to his brother. He carried the baby on his back, and went home the way he had come. While he traveled, the baby grew fast. She grew to be a girl, and Coyote wanted to marry her. When Coyote got home he said to Wolf, "This girl is my wife." Wolf, who knew everything, said "Shame on you. That is your daughter, not your wife." Coyote said, "Oh, yes, she is my daughter. I was just fooling."

In the morning, Wolf said, "Let us go and kill some fresh meat for the girl." Coyote said, "All right." They went out to a high place in the mountains, where they killed a deer. Wolf said, "You skin it right here. Do it yourself, and don't ask the girl to help You." Coyote said, "All right. Oh, yes, I will do it myself." He started to skin the deer, and then called the girl to help him. He told her how she should cut through the skin and fat. While she was cutting it, she shook some blood from her knife. When Coyote saw this, he said, "Oh, you are bleeding. You shouldn't eat meat, it will make you old and wrinkled. You should work hard and carry lots of wood, then you will live to be old. Now go off and get some wood." This scolding made the girl angry, but she said, "All right, I will get some wood." She went off and did not return.

Wolf came to Coyote, and said, "Where has the girl gone?" Coyote said, "Oh, she has gone after some wood." Wolf said, I know. You scolded her. You wouldn't let her eat any of her meat. Now she is angry and has gone away and left you." Coyote said, "Yes, that is right, I scolded her." Wolf said, "She has gone way up in the mountains to the north." He told Coyote where she had gone. He said that she had met Mountain Sheep, who was a handsome young man, and he had taken her to live in a cave in the mountains.

COYOTE LEARNS TO FLY (LIDA, NEVADA. SHOSHONI)

COYOTE and his brother Wolf had a camp in the Shoshoni Mountains. They had no baskets. Wolf asked Coyote to get some willows and make a basket. Coyote found the willows, cut them down, and rolled them up in a bundle. He heard a noise like singing, but he did not know where it came from. He looked and looked for the source of the singing. He put his willows on his back and departed from Wolf's camp.

Coyote soon began to dance with the willows on his back. He said, "Now I am a doctor." He asked some seeds on the ground, "How do I look while I am dancing?" He still heard the singing. Finally, he looked up in the air and saw some Geese who sang as they flew. Coyote called to them, "Which way are you going? Wait, boys, I want to go with you." But the Geese said, "No; we cannot take that Coyote along." Coyote continued calling to them to wait for him, but, they started to fly north. Coyote then took the willows from his back and followed them, singing as they sang.

The Geese tired of having Coyote follow them. They stopped to wait for him to see what he wanted. They sat on some little round hills and waited. Soon Coyote came up to them, panting and sweating. He said, "I am tired. Each of you, give me one of your feathers and I will stick them in my arms and fly as you do." Each gave him one of his feathers, and he stuck them along his arms.

The Geese said to Coyote, "When you fly, go down to that little hill and stop there. Be sure to sit down facing away from us." Coyote said, "All right, I will."

Coyote ran along the ground, flapping his wings. His feet rose from the ground a little way. Then he rose higher and higher in the air. He was flying. He flew down to the little hill the Geese had indicated, but when he lighted on it, he faced the Geese. At this they became angry. They went to Coyote and smashed his head with rocks. Coyote died.

When Coyote awoke, he was lying on his back. He stretched himself and as his hands passed over his head he felt something soft near his head. He thought the Geese had left him mush to eat. He ate it with his fingers. Then he sat up. He felt his head and found that there was a large wound in it, and that he had eaten his brains, thinking they were mush. He vomited.

Coyote stood up and saw that the Geese were far away over the mountains. He said to himself, "I will travel on." He followed the Geese to the mountains, but when he arrived at the summit, he found that they had crossed the next range and were still far ahead of him over another range. He followed them to that range, and saw that they were over the summit of the Sierra Nevada Mountains. When he came to the summit of the Sierra Nevada Mountains, he could not see the Geese anywhere.

Coyote started down into the valley, but at the canyon mouth he saw many Indians lying dead. He looked at them all but every one was dead. He saw one, woman with a large belly, but she too was dead. He took his knife and cut her belly; inside, he found a little baby girl. He said to this girl, "You are my sister. Yes, you must be my little sister."

Coyote made a willow cradle for the baby. He tied her to it, and told her, "We are going to my brother's camp." He carried her on his back, and started out. On the journey the girl grew very fast. Coyote called her his sister all the time. The girl was walking before they reached Wolf's camp.

When Coyote arrived at Wolf's camp he left the girl, who was now a young woman, outside the camp and went in to see Wolf. Coyote said "I have a wife. I left her outside the camp." Wolf said, "That is not your wife, that is our sister. Bring her into camp." Coyote said, "No, that is not our sister. That is my wife." Wolf said, "She is our sister," and he went out and brought her in. He gave her a place to sit.

The girl stayed for a little while, and then wanted to go back home. As she was leaving, Wolf gave her a stick painted white. He said to her, "Take this stick and when you are a short distance from camp, throw it over your head. Then turn around and look and you will see something." The girl put the stick on her back, and walked away. When she had traveled a short distance, she threw the stick over her head. She turned around to look and saw that it had become a little boy. This was her brother. She took him with her and they returned to their home.

When they had been there a little while, the girl cut some willows and made two baskets. One was very good and finely woven. The other was a poor basket. The girl gave them to the young boy and told him to take them back to Wolf's camp. She told him to give the good basket to Wolf and the poor one to Coyote. She also told him not to go into any caves. This boy was Coyote and Wolf's nephew (nadabu, "sister's son").

While the young man was traveling to Coyote's camp, a heavy rain started to fall. He saw a cave ahead. He said, "I am not going to sleep out tonight and get wet." He went into the cave, and spent the night there. In the morning he stood up and bumped his head on the roof of the cave. He found that he, had two big horns. He said, "I am a mountain sheep." He left the baskets in the cave, and jumped out on top of some big rocks by the cave. He said, "Now I know I am a sheep." He found two other sheep. They went with him to Coyote's and Wolf's camp. This Mountain Sheep, Wolf's nephew, had some beads around his neck.

When the Sheep approached the camp, Coyote said, "We must go out and kill that ram." Wolf said, "No, that is our nephew." Wolf saw the beads around Mountain Sheep's neck.

There were two brothers, also Wolf's and Coyote's nephews, who lived in the air, directly above the camp. They, too, saw the Mountain Sheep. The younger brother said to the older, "We must kill that ram." The older said, "No, that mountain sheep has beads around his neck. That is Coyote's nephew." The younger brother did not believe this, and continued to talk all day, asking the older brother to help him kill the ram. The older brother finally became tired of hearing the younger talk, and said, "All right. Go down and kill him." After the younger brother had killed Mountain Sheep, he saw the beads around his neck. He was sorry, because he knew then what he had done.

The younger brother said to the older one, "I am dry as a fish. [1] I want some water." Both went down to the spring to get a drink. Wolf asked Spider to make a fire. He asked Spider to put heavy rocks in it, so that they would get hot. Spider did as he was told. While the two brothers from the sky were drinking at the

---

[1] The simile is not obvious; and almost certainly is not native.

spring, Spider hit both of them with the hot rocks from the fire. Then he crawled inside them and killed them.

Wolf was singing, "Our nephew has been killed. Dig a hole and bury him there." Coyote said, "What kind of brush shall I use?" Wolf cried, and, finally, Coyote cried.

COYOTE LEARNS TO FLY (BIG SMOKY VALLEY, NEVADA. SHOSHONI)

GOOSE said to Coyote, "I'll give you wings. See those two sharp mountains? One is farther away. If I give you wings, you can fly up to that hill." Coyote said, "All right."

Goose pulled some of his feathers out and stuck them along Coyote's arms and said, "If you fly, sit on that mountain and wait for me. Don't go away. I will watch you." Goose sat down to watch. Coyote said, "All right," and went, saying "Wa' wa' wa'." He felt good. He said, "I don't want to sit on that hill. I feel good." He flew a long way and fell down.

Goose was watching him and found him. He went to Coyote and broke his head. Coyote's brains ran out and he died.

When he came to life he felt his brains and said. "My nephews gave me some mush." He ate some. Then he found that his head was broken and that he had been eating his own brains. He vomited. Goose came and found him and said, "You are bad, adabu!" He took his wings away from Coyote and left him.

Coyote cried. He did not know what to do.

COTTONTAIL SHOOTS THE SUN (SALINE VALLEY, CALIFORNIA. SHOSHONI)

COTTONTAIL (Rabbit) and his old mother lived in a house in Saline Valley. One day Cottontail went out to kill Sun. He took all the arrows he could carry. He started off toward the east and slept on a hillside that night. When Sun came up next morning, it poked Cottontail on his back to tease him. That is why Cottontail's back is yellow.

Cottontail saw that Sun had come up on a mountain farther to the east. He went over there. Next day he saw that Sun had come up on a mountain still farther to the east. He went over there. In this way Cottontail continued to go toward the east until he came to the edge of the ocean. He saw that Sun came up from the ocean and jumped up into a tree.

Cottontail went to the tree, and stayed under it to watch for Sun. He looked around for wood that would not burn (presumably to make his arrows). He was afraid that he would get burned and made a hole to hide in. Then he killed Sun with his bow and arrow, and jumped into his hole. When Sun fell to the earth, everything was burned.

After awhile, Cottontail reached out and felt the ground. It was still hot. He said, "tcuwa, tcuwa" and went back into his hole. He stayed there a long time.

When the ground was cool, Cottontail came out. He killed Sun, took its gall out, and threw it high up in the air. As Cottontail traveled home, people would tease him and say, "Look at

Cottontail. He is a big man. He has killed Sun." They laughed at him. This made Cottontail so angry that he killed everyone he met.

Cottontail walked for many days and finally arrived home in Saline Valley where his mother was waiting for him. They lived in a big brown rock which today is called "Cottontail's house."

COTTONTAIL SHOOTS THE SUN (ELKO, NEVADA. SHOSHONI)

AT one time the sky was too low; it burned everything. The people would say "üdü üdü üdü, it is too hot."

Cottontail said that he would kill Sun. He and Sand Rabbit walked toward the east. They went over mountains, mountains, mountains, mountains. Always the Sun came up over the next mountain to the east. They went over many mountains. Finally, they came to the big water and could go no farther. Here they stopped.

Cottontail told Sand Rabbit to make a tunnel, to make the tunnel twist in every direction, to make it go down, and go this way and that way and up and down. Sand Rabbit did not listen to his, brother and made the tunnel his own way. He made it straight. Cottontail made a tunnel that twisted in all directions.

Cottontail and Sand Rabbit stayed in their holes all day. Sun came up but they did not come out. They stayed in their holes for 7, 8, or 9 days.

Cottontail had many arrows that he was going to shoot at Sun. When Sun came over, he made ready to shoot. He shot at Sun and then jumped back in his hole. But the arrow burned up before reaching Sun. He had plenty of arrows and shot them all; but they all burned up and did not hit Sun. Then Cottontail took a roll of sage bark (i. e., slow match) that was about as long as from his fingertips to his elbow. He shot this at Sun. Sun fell down dead. When Sun came down there was a great conflagration. Everything caught fire and water boiled all over the earth. Cottontail had jumped back into his hole and kicked dirt behind him to keep out the fire. Just enough fire got to him to burn his neck, wrists, and ankles. Sand Rabbit had only dug down about 6 inches under the ground in his straight hole. He was roasted to death.

Cottontail wished to make a new Sun. He cut out Sun's gall and tried to make a new Sun of it, but it had green spots on it, so he made the moon out of it. Then he took Sun's bladder and made a new Sun of it. It had two holes in it where he had shot through it, but he patched them up and made a fine, new Sun. Sand Rabbit lay dead while Cottontail made the new Sun. Sand Rabbit had burned to death.

Cottontail pushed the sky up with his head and then threw the now Sun up to it. The sun was no longer too hot.

The sun went west and Cottontail started west, too. He was lonesome. He was ashamed and kept his head down.

After a while, Cottontail came to some people who had no mouths. They had a fire, and leaned their faces over it to inhale grease through their noses. Their noses were all black. Cottontail took a piece of flint and cut a mouth on one of them. After this, they all took flint and cut each other's mouth. They all began to talk.

Cottontail left these people and went on alone toward the west. After a while, he heard someone yelling and shooting. There was snow. He made tracks in it under rose bushes. Then he made a long hole, about 300 feet long. One person said, "Here are Cottontail's tracks." Another one said, "There are his ears. I can see them sticking up out of that hole." They all made fun of him. One said, "I am the best shot. Let me shoot him." They quarreled about who was to shoot him. Someone aimed at Cottontail, but as soon as he released the arrow, Cottontail jumped down his hole. They looked everywhere for him, but could not find him.

Cottontail went on toward his home. His sister was there. When he arrived, he asked her for some of the paint that she used on her face. He wanted to paint his own face. He took the paint and made stripes around his eyes. Then he went into a house where there were some girls. He sat opposite the door. When the girls' brothers came home, they looked in the house and saw Cottontail with the paint on his face. They were afraid to come in, and said, "ünü ünü ünü ünü." Then the girls said, "Take that paint off your face and let our brothers come in. Wipe it off."

The boys came in and pushed Cottontail around toward the door. He took the girls on his lap and held them.

They all roasted cottontail rabbits in the fire, a big fire in the middle of the house. Each person had a cottontail rabbit. After the rabbits had cooked for a while, Cottontail took a piece of rye grass and shot it into his roasted rabbit's head. He dragged the rabbit out of the fire. The others shot, as Cottontail had done, and dragged their rabbits out. When Cottontail started to cut open his rabbit, he wished that all the f at on the other rabbits were on his own. When be cut open its belly, the fat was fine and thick. When the others cut their rabbits open, they were skinny without any fat.

After this, all the people remained around the fire and sang until late in the evening. Then they all tried to go to sleep, but Cottontail sang, "Tu, tu, tu, tu, tu, tu," in a squeaky voice. The girls said, "You keep still and let our brothers go to sleep."

The girls were lying by the door. The boys were lying on the other side of the house. When everyone was asleep, Cottontail tied the long braids of each boy to those of the boy next to him. Then he set fire to the house and carried out all the girls under one arm. The girls said, "You are no good. You have burned up our brothers." This made him angry, and he threw the girls into the fire.

Cottontail came on from that place. He came along and along and along. He found an old woman making a basketry water jug. He said to her, "Mother, let me try that. Old Lady, let me try." He took the basket; then he gave it back to her; then he took it again. They exchanged it every few minutes. Cottontail wove the jug with the woman inside. He left her there. She died, and he went on his way.

Cottontail was lonesome. As he traveled along, some people looked at him and laughed. They said, "Oh, look at Cottontail. He killed Sun. He is a funny little short fellow. He killed Sun!" Cottontail looked up and saw that there were some pretty women in the rocks above him. He went up toward the rocks, and the women said, "Cottontail is ugly. He is coming up here." They all ran into cracks m the rock. Cottontail was angry. He found some brush and put it in all the cracks. He set fire to it. The women called, "Cottontail"; but none of them came out. Cottontail said to them, "You will be good to eat. You will be groundhogs. My people will eat you when you turn into groundhogs."

Cottontail went on. He thought, "What am I doing? I have no friends. I am all alone." He kept on traveling and saw many snow birds (gaim). He killed 8 or 10 of them. After this he came to Coyote. Coyote said to him, "Where did you get the birds? I am hungry. I want some." Cottontail said, "I pulled out my hair here" (indicating his pubic hairs) "and tossed them out. They turned into birds and I got them. Do not try to get too many." Coyote pulled out a few hairs, and they turned into birds. He picked them up. Then he tried to get some more, but pulled out his guts and killed himself.

Cottontail went on. He walked slowly; he was coming away, coming away, coming away, coming away. He found two girls digging roots (nap:). He made himself small, like a water baby, and walked toward them. He staggered. The girls said, "Look at this." They picked him up, and held him close in their arms, like a baby, to keep him warm. They fed him and were very good to him. That night they kept him between them to keep him warm. He felt at their breasts to try to get milk. He tried all night to nurse them. In the morning they cooked roots (nap:) for him, but it was too hard and he could not eat it. He wanted to nurse the girls; he wanted milk. He felt them again, but there was no milk. The next night Cottontail tried again to get milk from the girls, but they did not have any.

The girls' camp was near a spring with a hill behind it. In the morning Cottontail said, "Where is your digging stick? I want to dig some roots. Give me your big stick." The girls said, "It is too heavy for you." Cottontail said, "No." He dragged the big stick along; he was not strong. He fell over trying to drag it. He pulled the stick out of sight over the hill, and began to dig a ditch. He dug it all the way around the camp and then turned the ground [i. e., the entire camp] over and killed the girls.

Cottontail came on toward the west. He came a long way. He was coming in this direction. He crossed a hill and met some men whose hair was all shaved off except on their pates ["like Chinamen"]. He said to them, "Friends. You are my friends." He did not stop with them, because he thought that he must be good to them. He went on past these men and did not harm or kill them.

Cottontail continued to come west. He came to where there were Rattlesnakes. He saw them, but went on past. Rattlesnakes tried to shoot him. Cottontail became angry and killed them. He roasted them in a fire, and said, "You will be rattlesnakes, out in the hills, but not in the valleys." [1]

Cottontail went on and found two boys camped by a creek. The boys said, "Here is our brother coming." They called him ăŋgatasump: [ăŋga, "red," + tasump:, "a plant"], a flattering name. They said to him, "We are having a difficult time with this water here. It fights us. The wood fights us and drops on us. The willows make trouble for us." Cottontail said, "You try them again and I will see." The boys tried to get water, but it turned into ice. Cottontail shot it. They tried to get willow sugar (suhuviha), but the willows dropped on their heads. Cottontail remedied that. These boys were Hummingbirds. Cottontail said, "That is a good name they called me. It is the first time I have been spoken to pleasantly." [2]

Kaŋgwusi gweak: (Wood rat's tail, pulled off).

---

[1] B. G. said that he had probably omitted one or two episodes in this portion of the story.
[2] B. G. regarded this as the Shoshoni classic, the one important myth that explained everything, the "Shoshoni bible."

THE LENGTH OF WINTER; COYOTE IS BITTEN (SALINE VALLEY, CALIFORNIA. SHOSHONI)

COYOTE, Owl, and Whippoorwill (To'ovego) were making the year. Coyote was fixing the length of winter. Coyote said, "It should have as many months as the hairs on my back." Owl said, "No, it should have as many months as my feathers." "No, there are too many feathers and hairs," Whippoorwill said, "it should be 4 months." He flew away singing, "Watsa mu'a (4 months)."

Coyote became angry, and ran after Whippoorwill, but could not catch him. While Coyote was following Whippoorwill, he came to some red berries (puhupuhya). As he sat eating them, a rattlesnake bit him. He wanted to tell somebody that he had been bitten. He found a man, and told him to tell the people. The man went a short distance and came back. Next time he went farther and camp, back. He kept doing this until he finally got tired. Coyote died while the man was going back and forth.

HAWK AND THE GAMBLER (SALINE VALLEY, CALIFORNIA. SHOSHONI)

HAWK (Tuhu'ni) and his sister-in-law, Snow Bird (Takandado'a), were the only people left in the world. Everyone had gone to Panamint Valley (Hauta) to gamble, but none of them had come back. All the animals--Coyote, Wildcat, Bear, Crow, and others-- had gone and had been killed.

Hawk lived alone. He asked his sister-in-law to come and live with him, but she refused. She would not go near his house.

One day Hawk disappeared. When he did not return Snow Bird went to look for him. She looked in his house and found that he had jumped out through the hole in the roof. She walked around and around looking for his tracks. When she found them, she began to follow him. She followed him a long way and finally caught up with him.

When Snow Bird overtook Hawk, he said, "Why do you follow me? I am going over where I will be killed. You had better go back." She said, "No, I will go with you." Hawk asked her if she were brave. He asked her to sing. She began to cry, singing "Hovía, hovía, pasáqwai yumákan:". Hawk said, "What power have you to protect you from danger?" She said, "You see that mountain with snow on it?" The snow was clear like ice. "That is my power. It will help me." Hawk said, pointing to a mountain, "That is tuhu toyavi" (tuhu, "black," + toyavi, "mountain"). "That mountain is my power and will help me."

She went close to him, and they walked along together. He sang, "Tuhukini nuwu pasai yani pasai yani," and repeated it again and again."[1] Snow Bird also sang her song. They went along toward the home of the Gambler singing their songs.

The Gambler (Pano''wazⁱ) had killed all of Hawk's and Snow Bird's people. He lived with his many daughters and with two Gophers, who were Hawk's mothers-in-law.

Late in the afternoon, Hawk and Snow Bird came near to the place of the Old Man, the Gambler. Gophers saw them coming when they were far off and started out to meet them. Gophers took them to their house. While traveling to the Gambler's place, someone had warned Hawk and Snow Bird that the Old Man would offer them food, but that they should not take it, because it would be poisoned. All night Hawk stayed awake, because the Old Man waited to kill him. The Gambler would say, "Is he asleep?" Hawk would hear him, and say, "No, I am not asleep."

In the morning the Gambler's daughters began to grind acorns. They ground a great many acorns so that they could have mush. The old man said, "Grind them well, because we are going to have mush with Hawk meat for breakfast."

Hawk and the Gambler began a kick-ball race.[2] They kicked their balls around a long course. Gambler took the lead and remained ahead. The two old women, Gophers, were going to help Hawk. They made holes in the course, so that the Gambler

---

[1] The tune is nearly identical with that In the Owens Valley Paiute versions. (See footnote 2, Steward, J. H., Myths of the Owens Valley Paiute, p. 438, 1936.)

[2] This is the only record of this game. Informants denied that these Shoshoni had ever played it.

stumbled and fell in them. Meanwhile, Hawk had made one of his eggs into a ball, and used it instead of the one given him by the Gambler. The Gambler did not see him exchange the balls. With the help of Gophers, Hawk beat the Gambler.

Near the goal they had built a big fire in which to burn the loser. When the Gambler was beaten, he said, "You have beaten me. Take, my money and everything I have." Hawk said, "No, I did not agree to that." He wanted to kill the Gambler and all his people. Hawk said to the Gambler, "Sharpen your knife well and kill your people." The Gambler was rubbing the dull edge of his knife on their throats, saying, "Hwi, hwi," in a squeaky voice. Then Hawk took the knife from him and killed the old man and his daughters.

During the race, Snow Bird had been sitting close to the fire. After the Gambler and his people were killed, Gophers went to Snow Bird to carry her away, but she had grown roots so that if the Gambler had won the race and had attempted to throw her into the fire, he would have fallen in, instead. The old women continued to lift, and after a while, pulled up Snow Bird, roots and all.

Hawk saw all his own people piled up. They were dead and Coyote was among them. They had lost their arms, legs, heads, or other parts of their bodies. Coyote said, "Make a leg for me right away, before you fix anybody else." Hawk restored all the people.

THE FLOOD (SALINE VALLEY, CALIFORNIA. SHOSHONI)

AT one time the world was filled with water. Only the Inyo MOUNTAINS were left above it. All the people went to the summit of these mountains. (Probably New York Butte.) The water ran off toward the south.

RAT AND MOUNTAIN SHEEP (SALINE VALLEY, CALIFORNIA. SHOSHONI)

RAT (Kawa) had a home on the top of a mountain, [1] where he was building a dance corral. When he finished the corral, he went out to hunt Mountain Sheep.

Rat stood on a mountain, calling in his own language, "Nikadawa piwiavi, nikadawa piwiavi," inviting the Mountain Sheep to come join his circle dance and have a big feast. The Mountain Sheep answered "Hoho''°." That night the Sheep came to his dance. When they arrived, Rat began to sing his circle dance song in a monotone:

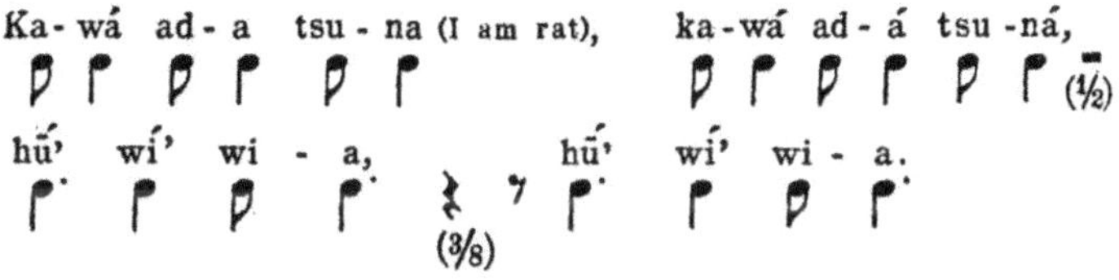

Ka- wá ad - a   tsu - na (I am rat),   ka -wá ad - á tsu -ná,

hǘ' wí' wi - a,   hǘ' wi' wi - a.

(⅜)   (½)

He picked out the largest of the Mountain Sheep and said to him, "You are my friend. I want to dance close to you." Then he said to all the Mountain Sheep, "Carry your babies with you on your backs while you are dancing." He told them all to shut their eyes while they were dancing. Rat sang his dance song and they danced all night. When it was nearly morning, while the people had their eyes shut, Rat stabbed the big Mountain Sheep that was dancing next to him. He killed him. Then Rat shouted, "Who

---

[1] Tucki Mountain, southwest of Bungalow City, according to W. P.

killed that man? It must have been a Wavitc."[1] The people opened their eyes and looked around. They all began to cry. Rat leaned his head on his hand and said, (crying in a falsetto) "Tana ho nano ho' budi." Then Rat said to the people, "Well, you people can go home now. I'll put this man into a fire and burn him up. After that, I will go home."

The Mountain Sheep went home. When they were gone, Rat, who was left alone, skinned Mountain Sheep and dried all the meat.

When Rat had eaten all his meat, he went out again and called the Mountain Sheep as before. Again they answered and came down to his dance that night. He told the biggest one to dance close to him and the others to dance with their babies on their backs and their eyes closed. But this time the Mountain Sheep said, "It is probably Rat who is doing this. Tell the children to watch him while we dance." The children watched Rat while they danced and saw him stab the Mountain Sheep next to him. Then Rat ran for his bow and said, "Where is the Wavitc who is doing this stabbing?" After the people had left, Rat cooked the Mountain Sheep he had stabbed.

When Rat had no more meat, he went into the mountains and called the Mountain Sheep as before. They answered and came down to his dance. Again he asked the biggest one to dance beside him and told the others to carry their babies and keep their eyes closed. But while they were dancing, the Mountain Sheep next to Rat stabbed him in the belly. Rat ran away and the people ran after him. They looked for him in his hole but could not find him. While they were looking, they found Mountain Sheep meat that he had dried.

---

[1] The Indians to the south of the Shoshoni; Wavitc = "tough."

COTTONTAIL AND WIND (SALINE VALLEY, CALIFORNIA. SHOSHONI)

COTTONTAIL lived with the people on the side of Olancha Peak. The people had no wind; there was none in the whole valley. They could hear it up on the top of the mountain, but it never came down.

Cottontail said, "I can bring the wind down the valley." He took a flute and went way up on the mountain side, blowing it "tu hú du dù du dù, mi áh" and singing "tavotsikita wo bü hai yuvü" (in effect, "I am Cottontail"). [1]

By means of his flute playing and his singing, Cottontail brought the wind down to the people in the valley.

---

[1] The tune is approximately that of Cottontail's song in "Coyote and Cottontail," by T. S. (See footnote 2, Steward, J. H., Myths of the Owens Valley Paiute, p. 437, 1936.)

THE DEER STEALER (DEATH VALLEY, CALI-FORNIA. SHOSHONI)

MANY people had houses at a camp where they were hunting deer and all kinds of animals. All the animals were people at that time. There were Eagle, Bullet Hawk (Kini'i), Red Tail Hawk (kwiyo'o), Crow, Coyote, and all kinds of birds and animals.

The people were hun. ng deer. Each night they brought home meat. When they brought it home they saw that a small kind of fly (Pakū'wund) [1] stole it. They went hunting again and brought home a whole, unbutchered deer. Pakūwund came back. He flew along, lit on the deer, and flew away with the whole thing. The next morning they went hunting again. When they came home, they tied two deer together by their legs and laid them side by side, Pakū'wund returned, lit on the deer and carried both of them away. The people went hunting again the following morning. That night they tied three deer together by their legs. Again Pakū'wund came, lit on them, then carried away all three.

Coyote spoke. He said, "Some of you had better watch that thing and see where it goes." Hawk (tuhun:) started to follow it. He walked over the hill and when he was out of sight pursued Pakū'wund. He saw him go toward the South and followed him to some clay hills. Pakū'wund went into a hill. Hawk knew then where his home was. He started back home. He lit on the other side of the hill from his people's camp, so that they would not

---

[1] "Something like a small animal."

see him, and walked into the village. He told them that he had followed Pakū'wund into the clay hills. The people said, "That is all right."

Coyote, who was chief, started to talk. He said, "We'll see about this in the morning." In the morning, all the people went south to the clay hills. They stopped there. There was a little hole in the top of the hill. The Pakū'wund was inside, but the people were not sure of this. They decided to smoke him out and began to gather wood. They built a fire and blew the smoke to drive it into his house. They did this all day. Coyote said, "Let me try." He blew, ran out of breath, and fell down the hill. After a while he blew again, ran out of breath, and fell down the hill. He did this again and again. After this the people began to dig. They thought they had killed Pakū'wund. When they had dug deep enough, they reached in to their deer meat and began to pull it out. Some of them said, "We had better leave it alone. He might not be dead. He might come and kill us." They came back from the place and left Coyote there alone.

Coyote said, "I shall go in and see him myself." Coyote started to dig. He reached in to the house and found that Pakū'wund's children were all dead. Pakū'wund came out carrying a stone pestle (paku'u) in his hand. He came out to where Coyote had reached into the hole. Coyote jumped to the top of the hill, where they had started to dig. Pakū'wund jumped after Coyote and struck at him, but Coyote dodged and he missed. Pakū'wund swung again, and Coyote said, "I am not going to dodge the same way every time. I will jump the other way." Pakū'wund knocked Coyote down and killed him. He chased the other people. First he caught Lizards and Snakes and the others that were running slowly. He killed them. He killed each of them as he came along. The birds were faster, but he caught and killed them. He killed Crow, Panzaya [some kind of hawk that catches ducks] and Kwiyo'ᵒ (?). Then he killed Eagle. There were only two persons left. They said, "We had better go faster to our house." Pakū'wund chased them. Hawk (Kini'ⁱ) said, "I cannot go much farther. I am tired." Pakū'wund killed him. There was only one person left, also Hawk (Tuhun:). He started to sing. He was on the other side of the Sierra Nevada mountains, west of Lone Pine. He said, "I am going to where my pond is." He headed for the water, darted into it, and then out again. Pakū'wund did the same thing, close behind him. Hawk made a turn, dove into the water again and came out. Pakū'wund dove in after him and out close behind him. Hawk said, "I am going to my house." He started toward his house, which was in a rock. This rock was Mt. Whitney. He went through his house and out the other side. When Pakū'wund could not get through the rock, he struck it with his pestle, broke it, and continued to follow Hawk. Hawk made a turn, then pulled a short feather from the upper part of his wing, near his shoulder. He put it in front of his house, then passed through and looked back. He could not see Pakū'wund, who had been caught between the feather and the rock.

Hawk went up on top of Mt. Whitney and spread his wings to rest. He was very tired.

Hawk had sung his song while Pakū'wund was chasing him.

THE SKY BROTHERS (DEATH VALLEY, CALIFORNIA. SHOSHONI)

MANY people had camps where they were hunting mountain sheep. Their chief went ahead and made fires (when they hunted).

There were two brothers in the sky (tugumbi, "sky"; duwitc, "boys"). They traveled along shooting arrows in competition with someone. [1] Doing this, the brothers lost all their arrows.

The brothers went to the camp of the sheep hunters; they went to the fire. When they arrived they had no arrows because they had lost them all. The people gave one arrow to each of the brothers, and said, "When you see a mountain sheep, the older of you must shoot it." All the people went hunting. The brothers went along together. They saw a sheep. The younger said, "I had better shoot him." The older one said, "No." The younger disagreed with him, and they argued. Finally, the older one yielded and said, "All right, shoot." The younger brother shot at the sheep, but did not hit it squarely, and the sheep ran away. When the people had given them the arrows they had said, "If you do not kill the sheep, do not chase it. You might get into trouble." The brothers argued. The younger said, "We had better track it." The older said, "They told us not to do that because we might get into trouble." The younger had his way, and they started to track the sheep. They followed its tracks. They came to a pool of water that was near somebody's house.

---

[1] They threw a bunch of willows ahead, over a bush where they could not see it, and shot to try to strike nearest to it.

The brothers went to the pool and took a bath. While they were bathing, they saw a sunshade built near the spring. After their bath, they went to the shade where some people lived. This was Snake's home. Snake said to them, "Tell me who you are." The brothers did not want to tell him. They said, "We heard that our grandfather lived here," though they really had no grandfather. [1] Snake said, "What are you two doing in this place?" The brothers said, "We have killed a sheep near here." Snake said, "All right, but you two must go back at once." Snake had two wives. He said, "If you don't go back right away, my wives will kill you."

Snake's wives were gathering berries (hu:pi). One of them began to sing. . . . She said, "I believe someone has come to our house." The other said, "You had better go on with your work." The first went on singing and said, "I tell you, someone has come to our house." She stopped picking berries and stood still.

Snake said to the brothers, "Where did you boys kill the sheep?" They said, "We killed it right there," and showed him the place. Snake said, "You must get a stick and throw me to where the sheep is. I will get it." They threw Snake with a stick and he landed by the sheep. Snake brought back the sheep. The boys went away. While Snake was carrying back the sheep, he covered up the boys' tracks so that the women would not see them when they came home. The boys went away to the sky. They sat there.

Snake used the mountain sheep's feet to cover up the tracks the brothers had made around the spring. Then he went to his house. The women were still gathering berries and one of them sang. After a while the other began to sing; they both sang. They said, "Someone came to our house."

---

[1] But compare below.

The women returned to the house. As they came near it, Snake had his head out of the house, looking toward the spring. The women knew that Snake was trying to deceive them. They said, "Someone gave him a sheep." Snake said to them, "Don't talk loudly. Some mountain sheep are watering at our spring." The women said, "Someone else killed this sheep." The women went to the water to bathe. They found a long hair in the water. It had become tangled around them. They compared the hair with their own and found that it was longer. They knew what had happened. They said, "Someone has come to our place." They sang . . . After their bath, the women walked around and around the spring to find the tracks of the person who had come. The brothers were above in the sky, watching them. The younger brother thought, "I hope one of them will look up and see us." The women looked up and saw the brothers sitting there. Then the women lay on their backs and sang. They said, "You had better come down." The younger brother said, "We must go down." The older said, "No, we will be killed." The two women had long knives. The brothers argued about it and at last the younger had his way. The older said, "You go down . . . and come back alive." The younger said, "I will go down . . ." He started down while the women watched him. When he came to them, they cut off his head. The older brother was very sorry when this happened, and said, "I, too, must go down and die." He went down and the women killed him. After they had killed the brothers, the women stayed there that night.

The next morning the people at the sheep hunting camp were talking. Bat had had a dream and told them about it. He said, "I dreamed last night that there was blood on the sky." Bat was the boys' grandfather, and when he said that he cried. He knew the boys had been killed.

That morning the women began to track the boys to see where they had come from. They followed the tracks to where they had shot the sheep, and then to where they had built a fire. They went on to the hunting camp. The people had their houses in a hollow. The women approached and looked at the camp from behind a ridge. Bat saw them looking toward the camp. When the women saw that Bat was looking at them, they went around the hill to another place and watched. Again they saw Bat looking toward them. Then they went around to another place. While they were doing this, they split juniper trees into small pieces with their knives. The pieces became people. They went toward the camp and the women accompanied them. The hunters saw them coming.

Coyote said, "Maybe they are going to have a fight with us. I am going to be out in front of everyone." He ran out in front of the hunters. The people came closer; Coyote was the first to have his head cut off. The people came on and cut off everyone's head. When they were through killing the hunters and were standing there, the women noticed that Bat was absent. They said, "Where is Bat, who was looking at us?" They searched for him among the dead people, and heard a noise like a mouse inside a mountain sheep carcass. They went to the sheep and found Bat hanging on the inside of the body. They took him out, and said, "This is our pet. We must take hill, home." Then they said, "Our husband might kill us. But our little Bat is pretty." They held him in their hands and made him fly. He flew around and lit on their heads. They said, "Our little pet is very good and pretty." They continued to do this. Bat flew around and lit on all parts of them. This made them angry and they tried to stab him with their knives but missed him. They continued to strike at him but stabbed themselves and died.

When the women were dead, Bat cut a piece out of each of them with a knife. He put both of the pieces around his neck like necklaces and started out for Snake's house. When he came to Snake, Snake said, "I know that you are wearing pieces of my wives." Bat said, "No, I won these a long time ago when I made a trip to the north. You were small at that time. You were in that cradle and I rocked you." Snake said, "No." He was angry and bit at a rock. Bat seized the shin bone of a deer and struck a rock with it. It made a red flash. He said, "I will do this to you, too." Snake became angrier. He was coiling, drawing himself higher and higher. Bat picked up a pebble and he flipped it into the air with his fingers. The pebble went high and as it fell became larger and larger. It fell on Snake's head and killed him.

Bat went back to where his dead grandsons were. He put a stick under one of them and threw him into the air. He came back to life. He did the same to the other boy, and he returned to life. He went back to his hunting camp and did the same to all the people who had been killed. They all came back to life. He did not do this to Coyote. Some people said, "We won't bother about Coyote. He always gets into trouble. We won't bring him back to life." But others said, "He is smart. He might tell us something." They threw Coyote up into the air with a stick and he came back to life. Coyote arose and said, "I have been sleeping."

ORIGIN OF DEATH (BIG SMOKY VALLEY, NEVADA. SHOSHONI)

WOLF said, "When people die, they must die twice." Coyote said "That isn't right. I don't want people to die twice. They must die once and be buried."

Wolf bewitched Coyote's boy and wished that he would die. Coyote knew that he had done this. The boy died. Coyote went to Wolf crying. He said, "Oh, brother, you said when people died they should get up and die again. When will my boy get up?" Wolf said, "Don't you remember saying they should die only once?"

COYOTE KILLS WOLF'S WIVES (BIG SMOKY VALLEY, NEVADA. SHOSHONI)

COYOTE hunted rabbits with the Indians. Coyote's brother, Wolf, had a wife. Coyote and Wolf hunted. When they returned home they found mush in baskets for them. Wolf's wife had left it for them, but Coyote could not see her. Coyote said, "What, is the matter? Where is my brother's wife?"

Wolf had a rabbit skin blanket. He slept under it. Coyote said, "Why does my brother leave that blanket there?" One day when Wolf and Coyote were hunting, Coyote sneaked back to the camp and saw a big Frog, Wolf's wife, under the blanket. It was she who had made the mush. Coyote said, "Oh, my, look what my brother has!" He killed her with a stick.

He went back to hunt. When Coyote and Wolf returned to camp, they found no mush in their baskets because Coyote had killed. Wolf's wife. Coyote said, "Oh, what are we going to eat, brother?"

Wolf and Coyote went hunting again. Wolf said, "We are going to move some place. Take everything. We will go to a place with water." They moved camp to a place where there was water. Coyote and Wolf hunted. When they returned home they found mush in baskets. Wolf's wife had made it, but Coyote, could see no woman. Coyote said, "What is the matter with my brother, talking to himself." Coyote sneaked back after they had started to hunt one day and saw the woman in the house. The woman went around the house and threw everything on top of it. Coyote said, "She is a pretty woman. I am going to catch her.

She is my brother's wife." He seized her. There were tiny red ants [evidently the wife or wives] going around the house. Coyote pinched them with his fingers and killed them.

Coyote went back to hunt with Wolf. When they returned to camp they found no food. All the women had been killed. Coyote cried because he was hungry. He said, "Oh, what are we going to eat, brother?"

BADGER, COYOTE, AND THE WOODCHUCKS (LIDA, NEVADA. SHOSHONI)

BADGER lived alone in his camp. He had lived there a long time. On a hill close by his home were some rocks. In these rocks were the houses of many Woodchucks (Yaha). [1]

Badger thought, "These must be very good to eat. I am going to try them." He sharpened a big stick on both edges; he had some kind of knife. Then he climbed up to the Yaha holes in the rocks. He found a flat place below the entrance to the houses and lay down there with his stick close beside him. He thought, "I will sing a song and pretend I am singing in my sleep." He started singing: He sang this song two or three times. Then he sat up and looked up to the rocks where the Woodchucks had their homes. A few had come out to look when he started singing. He thought "Maybe more will come out." He lay down again and continued singing. He thought, "I'll sing once more. Then I'll look again."

He sang the song twice more and then cautiously looked up. Many Woodchucks had come out to listen to him. They said, "Who is that singing? We will go down and see who is singing." Badger lay still with his head on the ground, and continued to sing. The Woodchucks said, "He has a very short tail." "What is

---

[1] J. S. explained that these Yaha were like rats or mice, but that he had never, seen any of them. Actually Yaha are woodchucks and, though an important food farther north, are unknown in this region.

that singing?" "His legs are very short, too." "Come and see what this is!"

Finally, many had come down to see Badger. Badger kept singing all the time. He didn't move at all. He kept his head down on the ground. He kept on singing. He held his stick down with his hand. The Woodchucks called up to those who remained on the rocks, "Come down and see what this is!" "He has very short ears." "It is hard to see his eyes. They are very small. He has a white spot on his nose." Badger continued singing all the time.

When all the Woodchucks were around him, watching him, Badger thought, "Now I have enough. I will knock them down with my stick." He jumped up quickly and began knocking the Woodchucks on the head with his sharp stick. He killed many of them. Only a few escaped, and ran back to their homes in the rocks. Badger thought, "I have plenty. I have enough."

He carried them on his back down to his camp and skinned then. They were very fat and good to eat. He dried the meat and made jerky of it. While he was skinning them he thought, "I have a lot of meat. These will be good to eat when they are dry."

When his meat was nearly all used up, Coyote came to see Badger. Badger had just made a stew of his meat. When it was cooked he gave Coyote some. Coyote said, "That is very good." He ate more; it tasted good. Coyote asked Badger, "What kind of meat is in that stew?" Badger answered, "That is not meat. I just pick them out of the rocks. They have a place up there. That is where I get them." Coyote said, "I am going to try to get some. How do you do it? Do you shoot them, or what?" Badger explained, "You just knock them down with a stick." Coyote said, "I'll bet I can catch more than you did. What kind of stick did you use?" Badger said, "Any kind of stick will do. It doesn't matter." Coyote said, "I am going to try it myself. I am going to lie up there, too."

Coyote made a stick for himself and then asked Badger, "What do you say to them while you are lying there?" Badger told him, "I sang a song, that is all." Coyote asked, "What kind of song? Can you give me the same song?" Badger gave him the song and Coyote practiced it. His voice was deep and hoarse and ugly. After he had practiced until he knew it, he went up to the rocks He looked around for a place to lie. He saw the holes of the Woodchucks and what he thought was a good place near them.

Coyote lay on his back. He started to sing Badger's song. It sounded bad. He only sang it once and then raised his head to look at the holes. There were no Woodchucks in sight. He sang once more and then looked again. No Woodchucks had come out. He thought, "I have been too impatient about looking up there." He sang the song two or three times and then looked. Some little Woodchucks had come out in front of their holes. They looked down to where Coyote lay. They said to the others, "Come out and look at this. It is a long one." Some of them went down to see better. They said, "This is a long one. What is it? It has a long tail." They called to the others to come and look.

More of the Woodchucks came down. Coyote had not stopped singing. They said, "He has a very sharp nose." "His ears are pretty long." More Woodchucks came out to look. Coyote thought, "I have plenty," but he wanted more to come down. He kept on singing.

The Woodchucks said, "We will touch him with our hands to see how that fur feels." They gathered around Coyote and put their hands on him to feel the fur. This tickled Coyote and he began to laugh. He frightened the Woodchucks and they all ran away. Coyote jumped up, grasped his stick and tried to hit them, but he missed every one. They were too far away. He didn't get one.

Coyote said, "I will try once more." He lay down again in the same place. He started to sing again. He sang the song twice and looked up. There was not one Woodchuck outside his hole. Coyote continued singing. He thought they would come out again. He sang the song five or six times, but no one came out to bear it. He thought he had better stop.

He got up and went to Badger's place. Badger saw that he had no meat. Coyote told Badger that the Woodchucks were too wild and had all gotten away. Badger said, "Yes?"

Coyote went home.

COYOTE AND THE BEAR CUBS; THE DEATH OF WOLF (ASH MEADOWS, NEVADA. SHO-SHONI.)

ONE day Wolf said to his brother, Coyote. "I would like some seeds. I like them better than meat. Go to your aunt's place and get some for me." Coyote said, "We have no relatives." Wolf said, "Yes; we have. You go over there and see."

Coyote went out to find the seeds and met two girl cousins, two bear cubs. They looked like twins. They were gathering seeds. Coyote talked to them for a little while. Then he choked both of them; they died. [1] He laid them side by side and covered them up with a rabbit-skin blanket. Then he started to gather seeds.

About sundown, Coyote's aunt, Bear, came to where the girls were. She was carrying seeds. She said, "What are you doing there, sleeping at this time?" She walked over to them, and pushed and pinched them, trying to wake them up. When they didn't move she looked under the blanket and saw that they were dead. This made her angry. She ran to Coyote and clawed all the meat off his back with her fingers. Coyote howled, "Wheeeeee." Then he ran away.

Coyote covered his back with a blanket and went home without his seeds.

---

[1] M. S. intimated that the girls rebuffed Coyote's amorous advances, which caused him to kill them.

When he arrived at his home, Wolf asked for the seeds. Coyote said, "I did not see any." Wolf, who knew everything, said "Yes, you did. Why do you cover your back? I know you killed those girls and your aunt clawed you." Coyote admitted that this was so.

Wolf wished Coyote asleep. He had this power. Wolf then went out hunting and killed a very small fawn. He cut the meat off its back in thin strips. It was very smooth and tender. When he got home, Coyote was still curled up asleep. Wolf slipped Coyote's blanket off and mended his back with the fawn's back muscles. He made it smooth, just like new.

In the morning, Coyote stretched himself and felt his back. He said, "My back meat has returned. Last night it was gone and there were just bones back there, but now it has come back. It is fine and smooth!"

Wolf said to Coyote, "Now you be good. You are always fooling me. Don't go back and bother your aunt. But, if you do, be sure to skin her and cut up all the meat and bring it home. Don't leave any of it."

Coyote said he would not go back, but he went nevertheless. He met Bear and cut her throat. He skinned her and cut up all the meat and wrapped it in the skin, but he forgot a piece of tripe. On the way home he remembered the tripe, and what Wolf had said about bringing all the meat home, so he went back for it. The Tripe had moved to the north. Coyote chased it but could not catch it. He asked, "What are you doing?" Tripe said, "I am well now. I am going to tell my people what you have done to my daughters." Coyote said, "Go ahead. I am glad."

When Coyote returned to the camp with the meat, he told Wolf he had brought it all home. Wolf said, "No you didn't. You had better watch out. When you see your people, you will find out why." Coyote said, "There are no people here. What is the matter?" Wolf only said, "In a few days you will see."

In a few days Wolf said to Coyote, "Stand away from the fire and look to the north." Coyote said, "Why should I? It is cold." But he looked, and in the north there was a crowd of people. They looked black in the distance. There was lightning. Finally Coyote said, "It looks like people coming closer. I can see arms and legs. You look, Wolf." Wolf would not look, but he said to Coyote, "You had better pack everything, and move away." Coyote said, "Why should I move?"

Wolf went out to see the people coming. The men in the crowd shot Wolf and he died. Then they skinned him, and taking the skin with them they went back to the north. Coyote was afraid, but he followed their tracks until he came to a big camp. The people had made things ready for a circle dance around a fire.

Coyote didn't dare go into the camp, but stayed on the outside, watching them. An old woman came up to him there and said, "Maybe you are Coyote." Coyote said "What is this Coyote?" The old woman said, "He lives at Tin Mountain (i. e., Charleston Peak), Coyote said, "What is he, a bad Indian?" She said, "I think you must be Coyote." He said, "I come from the north, but my grandfather told me about Coyote's brother, Wolf, who lives on Tin Mountain. Have you ever heard of him?" The old woman said, "Yes, my son has killed Wolf. My people have Wolf's hide. At sundown we will dance all night." The old woman then told Coyote that during the dance she tended the children of the dancers. She gathered them all around her and covered them all up with Wolf's hide. She said that was why she was crying. She told him that during the night while the children slept she, too, could dance a little, but in the morning the children would cry, "Mama, mama, come and take care of me."

When Coyote heard this, he had an idea. He killed the old woman. He beat her and beat her and broke all her bones. He then made a little opening in her skin and pulled all the bones out and made a sack. He climbed into this sack and looked just like the old woman. He took her stick and hobbled into the camp. The children all cried, "Grandma is coming." After sundown, the people all said, "Mama, look after the babies while we dance."

While the people were dancing, Coyote quietly choked the children to death. He held their noses, and choked them. The people thought the children were asleep and they asked him to dance. Coyote said, "All right." Then he jumped out of the old woman's skin and put on Wolf's hide. He ran out of the house shouting, "I am the man you killed," and then fled from the camp.

The people followed him, but he ran, ran, ran, ran, and finally came to a wooded mountain. Here the people lost the track and returned home. Coyote walked back to the place where Wolf had been killed. Wolf's carcass was all dried up and stiff like wood. Very carefully, he fitted Wolf's skin over the carcass.

In the morning he went out to look and saw that the nose had moved a little and was slightly wet. The next morning Coyote was awakened by hearing Wolf howl. He got up to look, but found that Wolf had gone to the northeast. Wolf was alive but he was very angry.

He left Tin Mountain and never came back. That is why there are no wolves or bears on Tin Mountain now.

POLE CAT, TAKADOA, AND HAWK (ELKO, NEVADA, SHOSHONI)

NIGHT Owl (Munibitc) lived with his wife and boy who was 6 or 7 years old. His wife, Takadoa, [1] carried the boy around on her back.

Night Owl went hunting for rabbits. While he was stamping his feet in the snow, he stepped on a piece of bone that was sticking up and drove it into his foot. He came home and asked his wife to pull it out. She wanted to marry Skunk, so she pushed the bone in farther and Night Owl died.

Takadoa went to Skunk's place and talked to his grandmother. She told her that she wanted to marry Skunk. The grandmother said that Skunk was strong, but was no good. She began to cry. Takadoa went away carrying her son. Skunk came home, and said to his grandmother, "What are you crying about, Grand-mother? Tell me what is the matter." She said, "Oh, I am just crying because my son has died"; she referred to Owl. Skunk said, "How do you know that he died? You must know some-thing." He smelled her. He said, "You are too old to smell this way." He smelled all around and knew that somebody else's smell was there. Then he found a string that had belonged to some stranger. Now he knew who had been there. He said, "Why didn't you tell me who was here?"

Skunk started to follow the woman, Takadoa. He followed her tracks. The woman thought, "I wish a lot of roses would grow up

---

[1] A black-headed bird that comes in the spring time.

so he can't get through." A lot of dry roses grew up and Skunk became stuck in them. Then Skunk looked up and saw an enormous alkali flat [i. e., playa] that had no end. Skunk let out his smell. It overtook the woman and her boy and killed both of them.

Badger, Coyote, Hawk (Kini), and their friends were camped on the other side of the flat. Badger restored Takadoa to life. She wanted to marry Hawk. She went to the camp and found that all the men were out hunting rabbits. Hawk's mother was alone. Takadoa saw only one bed in her house, but there were many rabbits there. After a while, Coyote came back with four rabbits. He gave them to Takadoa, and her boy, but Takadoa would not marry him. She wanted Hawk, but could not find him. Ha-wk was staying in a round hole up in the rocks.

Every evening someone brought a great many rabbits to Hawk's mother's house. Takadoa said, "Who brought all these rabbits?" Hawk's mother said, "My boy brings them." Takadoa looked all around and in the bed for Hawk. Hawk's mother said, "What do you want? Do you want my boy? After I die you want to marry him? No, you might make him trouble. You would scare him so that be could not hunt rabbits any more."

That night, after every one was asleep, Takadoa went to Hawk's place in the rocks to sleep with him. She went in the middle of the night. No one knew that she was going. When she arrived, she got in bed with him and called, "Kinini, kinini, kinini." When Hawk woke up and found somebody in bed with him he was frightened.

In the morning Hawk got up and sat on a rock with his feathers all ruffled. He looked funny. He went hunting for rabbits but only got one. His luck was spoiled. He had been the best of all hunters, but after being frightened by the woman, he was no good.

Kăngwasi gweak: (Woodrat's tail, pulled off).

COYOTE LIBERATES GAME ANIMALS; WOLF IS KILLED AND RESTORED (WINNEMUCCA, NEVADA. NORTHERN PAIUTE)

WOLF was our father. Coyote was Wolf's brother. Their home was in a cave south of Humboldt City. It is called "Wolf's house." Wolf had a hole [probably cave] in which he kept deer, sheep, buffalo, and antelope.

When Coyote went hunting he never found any game, but Wolf brought game home every time he went out. Coyote asked Wolf, "Where do you get game so quickly? Every day I look in the mountains but I do not even see tracks. Tell me, brother. Tell me how you get game so quickly." Coyote begged, begged, begged. Wolf said, "I keep the animals in a hole." "All right," Coyote said, "I will go and catch some." Wolf said, "Kill only one and then shut the hole up well." Coyote said, "I will."

Coyote went to the hole. But instead of doing as his brother had told him, he threw the door of the hole open and the deer, buffalo, elk, and others ran out. They ran, ran, ran. Coyote shot, shot, shot at them, but they ran past him. He could not kill any. The last animal to come out was a little fawn. Coyote killed that one.

Wolf looked out from his house and saw dust all over the mountains. All the game was gone. He knew that Coyote had let them escape. Coyote came back bringing his small deer. Wolf was very angry and lay down. He would not speak. Coyote said, "Brother, I have tender meat for you." Wolf would not speak.

Another tribe that lived in the north saw the dust in the hills and went after the animals. Wolf sent Coyote to get cane to make arrows. Wolf made the arrows very quickly. When they were finished, he put Coyote in the house and said, "I am going to fight [these people] alone. Don't look out of the house until I return." Wolf fought alone. He had told Coyote not to look out. Coyote did as he was told and waited. But after a while he looked out and Wolf was killed. The people from the north took Wolf's hide with his scalp inside it and went back toward the north. Coyote followed them. He saw where the people had put Wolf's scalp on a stick in the middle of their dance ground.

Finally, Coyote went over to the people. He cried when he saw his brother on the pole. He told the people, "The smoke from the fire follows me, around and makes me cry." He told them that they should dance for 5 nights without sleeping. The people said, "All right." They did not sleep day or night [during this time]. When everybody slept after the dance, Coyote took Wolf's hide and returned home. No one followed him because everyone was asleep.

On his way home, Coyote buried the hide in damp ground [each night when he camped]. On the third night he heard someone speaking. The voice said, "Coyote, make a fire." Coyote looked around but could see no one. He [went on and] camped again. In the morning he heard the voice say, "Coyote, make a fire." Coyote said, "My brother, my brother!" But he saw no one. When he was near home he heard the voice say, "Coyote, make a fire." Coyote said, "Brother, brother, brother." He caught Wolf's soul and brought it back. Wolf came back to life again.

THE ICE BARRIER (WINNEMUCCA, NEVADA. NORTHERN PAIUTE)

COYOTE and Wolf went to the north to fight. Many people went with them. Coyote had been to the Snake River alone [before this]. He gathered the people and went back there. Ice had formed ahead of them, and it reached all the way to the sky. The people could, not cross it. It was too thick to break. A Raven flew up and struck the ice and cracked it [when he came down]. Coyote said, "These small people can't get across the ice." Another Raven flew up and cracked the ice again. Coyote said, "Try again, try again." Raven flew up again and broke the ice. The people ran across [or through?]. They ran across. Coyote was the last person over.